CHRISTMAS DOWN UNDER

Australia, 1969: Manchester lass Pamela has given life in Sydney as a Ten Pound Pom a fair go, but since her husband ran off with a younger woman, she longs to return to the UK. However, when she books a one-way flight to take herself and her four-year-old daughter Sharon home by Christmas, it appears fate has other ideas. As Pamela's festive project at work takes off and she meets gorgeous but fashion-challenged teacher Nick, she begins to wonder whether life in Australia has more to offer than she'd thought . . .

ALAN C. WILLIAMS

CHRISTMAS DOWN UNDER

Complete and Unabridged

LINFORD
Leicester

First published in Great Britain in 2018

First Linford Edition
published 2019

A catalogue record for this book is available
from the British Library.

ISBN 978–1–4448–4294–4

Published by
F. A. Thorpe (Publishing)
Anstey, Leicestershire

Set by Words & Graphics Ltd.
Anstey, Leicestershire
Printed and bound in Great Britain by
T. J. International Ltd., Padstow, Cornwall

This book is printed on acid-free paper

1

It was going to be a momentous year for mankind — 1969. They were going to put men on the moon. It seemed so hard to believe — yet the Sixties had seen so many changes to the world, and my life in particular.

It would also be the year that Sharon and I would be starting our new life back home in England. I was looking forward to it so much.

Moving to Australia had been a mistake. Simply perusing the display of Christmas cards on the stand at our corner shop reminded me of how wrong living in Australia was.

'Hello. It's Mrs Grant, isn't it? And little Sharon, too. Going to buy some cards to send back home?'

I turned to see one of the parishioners from my local church, Mr McTavish. His Scottish accent reminded me that I

1

wasn't the only newcomer to Sydney. There were lots of us, brought out with promises of a new, better life to help populate this vast continent.

'Please call me, Pamela, Mr McTavish. As for the cards, it's only September. Every year they appear to begin the lead-up to Christmas earlier and earlier.' I paused, then pointed to a wintry scene on one with the strange wording *Happy Christmas From Down Under*.

'At least *you* can understand how having snow on Christmas cards just seems so wrong in this upside-down country we're living in.'

'Celebrating the birth of Our Lord is not a bad thing, Mrs Grant, even three months before the day. Nevertheless, I do understand. It's difficult to let go of traditions. Even Australians who have lived here for generations cling to British history and attitudes. Australia is a new country, less than seventy years old. It's still finding its way.'

I had to agree, yet that didn't stop

me from being frustrated. Forgetting for a moment that Sharon was with me, I pointed to another card.

'Look at this one, with Santa Claus in all his finery. If he came to Australia I'm sure he'd pass out from heat stroke and the reindeer wouldn't know what had hit them. As for flurries of snow — '

Mr McTavish glanced pointedly at Sharon. Instantly, I regretted my rash words. Like Noddy's best friend, my sweet daughter had big ears and had listened to my every word.

'Does that mean that Santa won't be coming this year?' she asked, clearly upset. I knelt down at her side to give her a reassuring hug.

'Of course not, sweetheart. Santa always comes to see the children of Australia. I imagine he'll change into a T-shirt and shorts, that's all.'

I had a vision of a portly Saint Nicholas in swimwear and tried to push it from my mind.

'You remember how hot it was here

last year, don't you, Sharon? We were both perspiring all day. In any case, we'll be back in England by Christmas and you'll get to see Grandpa and Grandma, Auntie Lorraine and all your cousins again.'

'But if we move away from Mrs de Luca's, Mummy, how will he know where I live?'

'Santa will know because he's special. And we'll write to him to remind him. You and me.'

That appeared to settle her apprehensions, at least for the moment.

It was difficult here without family support. At least, back in England, we could get on with our lives. Emigrating here hadn't been my idea, yet now we had to deal with the consequences.

I glanced around the shelves of the grocery store run by Mrs Comninos. There were so many product brands which I recalled from my own childhood, yet there were unfamiliar brands as well. Australia was a strange mixture, not only of new immigrants from countries in Europe including Britain, but a blend of ideas as well.

To me, Christmas in summer was totally wrong. It would make far more sense to hold it in July when it was winter in the Southern Hemisphere, but obviously that was never going to happen.

'Don't you miss the old country, Mr McTavish?'

'Of course I do. Nevertheless, Mrs McTavish and I are trying to begin a new life over here. We've made quite a few friends. There is one problem, though. The accent is so hard to understand. Dare I say it?' He gave a cheeky smile, the wrinkles on his face almost joining in. 'It's even worse than the way you English lassies speak.'

I grinned in agreement. Glaswegian accents were hard for me, too.

Just then, I caught a whiff of some odour that made my stomach muscles contract and my heart jump a little. It was coming from the Scotsman. I staggered backwards, causing a rack of magazines to tumble over.

'I'll sort it,' I hastily told the shopkeeper and Mr McTavish. There was no way I wanted him near me. Sharon helped me pick them up and replace in the wire stand.

'Are you OK, lass? You look like you've seen a ghost.'

I almost felt physically sick. 'There . . . there's some smell. I think it's coming from you.'

I hated to accuse him. It wasn't a nasty odour yet there was something that triggered severe nausea in me.

Mr McTavish stayed back, obviously concerned. He sniffed, then put his hands in his jacket pockets and removed some small white balls. He sniffed them and held them out. I drew back.

'Just a couple of mothballs, lassie. Nothing to be afraid of.'

Feeling stupid, I apologised. Clearly he didn't wear the jacket often.

I never used them. Hadn't smelled them in years. Why should they cause me to feel so ill?

I noticed that Mrs Comninos had finished serving her customer. We approached the counter with my shopping list at the ready. Mr McTavish politely kept his distance, clearly concerned about making me ill again.

Our lovely Greek shopkeeper took the paper and started to collect items from her shelves, placing them on the well-worn wooden counter.

'Mummy, can we have some Vegemite, please?' Sharon asked, tugging at my dress.

My eyes opened wide. Vegemite! It was black and smelled disgusting, though Sharon had taken a liking to it. Mrs de Luca put it on her sandwiches from time to time.

It was one of those strange parodies of proper British food. I wondered if we would be able to buy Vegemite in England. Some familiar treats might help Sharon adjust. Just as long as I didn't have to eat the gunge myself.

Encouraged by my reluctant assent,

Sharon had another request. 'Oh, Mummy. Could we have some chocolate for later, please?'

I asked Mrs Comninos for a bar of Dairy Milk. Even that had a different taste here.

We paid our bill and collected the loyalty stamps that Sharon loved to stick in the little book at home. Rather her than me. The taste of the glue was as vile as the Vegemite!

We made our way out of the shop and up the hill towards home. It was only a short walk, yet the gathering darkness made me hurry Sharon along. The mauve street lights were on, casting ghostly shadows on the footpath.

Sharon was four going on five, and yet she seemed far more mature than the other children I'd met occasionally. Perhaps it was something to do with me talking to her all the time like an adult.

My ex-husband had stranded us in this foreign country almost eighteen months ago. Frank had disappeared from our lives soon after arriving in Sydney, heading to Queensland with a fluffy-brained teenage girl. He'd hurt me — but worse, he'd hurt Sharon. She never mentioned him.

It was Friday night and I was looking forward to the weekend. Actually, there was a party to go to on Sunday which was highly unusual for me.

'Mummy. Why don't you like living in 'Stralia?'

Out of the mouths of babes. I realised just how tuned in Sharon was to my words and attitudes.

Maybe I was being unfair on my adopted country. I had an interesting, challenging job which was reasonably well paid for a woman. It was agreed from the initial interview that it would only last until December, which had suited me fine. I enjoyed it.

In some ways going back to England would be a step backwards for me. It was a sad fact that the male mentality over there would not allow me the employment chances that I'd had here.

However, England was my home. It's where I had grown up and probably where I would have stayed had I not met my ex.

It was true that I'd spent some years travelling around parts of Europe — though that wasn't the other side of the world. From here it took more than a day of flying, plus stacks of money, to even go home for a visit.

I tried to explain to Sharon about my feelings and where I felt most comfortable. It had been years since Mum and Dad had seen my little girl, years when she'd changed from a toddler into the inquisitive and gorgeous child she was now.

Phone calls were too expensive to make often, and invariably centred around the weather here and there. We never really chatted as we would if we were in the same room. Apart from work, there was nothing to keep me in Australia.

Dusk was far shorter in Sydney than

in Manchester. By the time we reached the gate through the paling fence surrounding Mrs de Luca's home, the creatures of the night had started their chorus. Crickets chirped and frogs croaked their sore-throat songs, all of which was quite comforting. The noise reminded me that we were not alone in the dark.

* * *

After dinner, we played some games, talking all the time while the radio played modern songs. Aussies loved their own pop groups, even supporting those who had moved to the UK, trying to break into the larger musical scene there.

Having Sharon to care for, I didn't pay much attention to songs these days. Still, I did recall seeing The Seekers once at a Manchester club. They spoke funny. Now I was surrounded by an entire country speaking with their nasal accents.

11

Glancing at the clock, I said it was bedtime.

'Can we read a story?' She'd donned her pink pyjamas and folded her daytime clothes neatly.

'Of course. Which one?'

Sharon had a number of Little Golden Books. I crossed my fingers that she'd choose anything but Cinderella. I knew it off by heart.

'Cinderella?' she replied. I struggled to maintain my happy face. My daughter giggled.

'I'm only joking, Mummy. I have a new one.'

She removed one of the series of readers from her school satchel. It was called *Mickey's Christmas Carol*.

'Mrs de Luca gave it me for being a good girl,' she proclaimed happily.

I smiled. My landlady was a treasure. Not only was she providing us with this small but cosy flat at the bottom of her garden, but she cared for Sharon when I was at work.

A Christmas story in September?

Why not? Nevertheless I couldn't help but feel like a female Scrooge. Happily another Christmas in Australia was unlikely . . . unless some unforeseen disaster screwed up my plans.

★ ★ ★

There were four rooms in our petite flat; a kitchen-diner-living area, a bathroom and the bedroom for Sharon and me, as well as another bedroom that was where we put all the unused clothes and games. We each had our own beds. I preferred to be close to my baby girl.

Sharon brushed her teeth and was soon snuggled up in bed. I was grateful that the nights were still cool enough to warrant a blanket. Again the thought of sleeping through a summer night above seventy-odd degrees was disconcerting.

We read the book together. Sharon recognised most of the words from other books and was beginning to learn individual sounds. I was so proud of her. She snuggled down under the blankets as I kissed her goodnight.

Even when I went to sleep, I'd leave a light on in the lounge with the bedroom door ajar. It was a childhood fear that I'd never lost.

I made myself a cup of tea. Even the brands were different over here. Lipton's seemed popular, although to me it tasted like sweepings instead of proper tea leaves.

Just then, I heard a quiet knocking on the front door and the sight of a flashlight moving around. It was Mrs de Luca.

I invited her in and offered her a coffee. It was what she preferred. Unfortunately it was the cheaper one mixed with chicory.

We both sat with our drinks.

'Apologies for disturbing you, Pamela. I am wondering if you and the little one would like to come with me to town tomorrow. I have a lay-by to collect.'

'Of course, but we'll have to leave early.'

It was another aggravating difference with Sydney. The shops closed at noon. How primitive — especially for workers like me who didn't have time on weekdays.

Mrs de Luca was a widow. Her son and family were spending a year back in Italy. She was lonely and would often drop by for a chin-wag, as she called it. She'd picked up a few Aussie expressions unfortunately, although I conceded she was at least trying to fit in.

After a friendly catch-up, she excused herself, saying it was late. As she switched her torch back on to cross the garden, she realised something.

'Oh, I nearly forget. Your mail.' She passed me two aerogrammes from her apron as she left. It had started to drizzle outside, but she only had twenty feet to go to reach her back door.

'I wish my Gino write as often as your family do, Pamela. Oh, and lock

15

up the house good and tight. There's talk of a burglar breaking in at night. We can't be too careful, Pamela. Buona notte. See you tomorrow.'

'So much for a Saturday lie-in,' I sighed after she'd left.

One letter was from my big sister, the other from Mum and Dad (but mostly Mum). I smiled. Ringing overseas on a trunk call was so expensive. Even with mail taking a week or two to arrive, aerogrammes — or better still, letters with photos — were a joy to receive here in the back of beyond.

My sister's news was always more detailed and juicy than Mum's. I knew it was a generational thing. It was the same with Mrs de Luca. I called her by her surname in deference to her age yet somehow felt uncomfortable when she used mine. I preferred being called Pamela, but I knew older people had enough to cope with in their lives without expecting them to give up traditional ways altogether. There had been the Depression, the war, followed by television and rock and roll music. Their world was altering very quickly.

Australia was far more judgmental about unmarried mothers than England these days. In spite of using my maiden name, I kept the title Mrs rather than Miss. In fact, Sydney was far behind in a lot of ways, fashion and attitudes being the main areas. My short dresses and swimwear had caused many an eyebrow to be lifted, and I'd even been asked to cover up at Bondi or leave the beach. Talk about embarrassing.

On my first day at work, to make a good impression I had worn a bouffant hairdo that was no longer fashionable back home. Dusty Springfield's innovative heyday of wearing that style was now ancient history but here in Australia it was still highly popular. Elsewhere the Sixties had moved on through an avalanche of change; Mods, Rockers and Oz's own contribution to peer group style . . . Surfers.

★   ★   ★

The following morning we met Mrs de Luca and made our way to the bus stop. The green and cream double deck bus wasn't long in coming.

A cheery conductor approached us with his ticket holder and cash bag over his shoulder.

'Two adults and a child to Town Hall, please,' I said, offering the correct change. It hadn't taken long for me to adjust to decimal currency, even their brightly coloured notes.

'From England? Just like me, luv,' he said, with a smile. His London accent was hard to miss.

'Manchester,' I replied, happily.

'Manchester, eh. Do they still wear clogs and shawls up there?' Suddenly our conductor wasn't such a pleasant man any longer.

'Naturally,' I replied. 'We are northerners after all. However we do have the most successful pop group in the world up our way — the Beatles. Don't suppose you've heard of them, 'luv'?'

Scowling, he handed us our tickets

and moved on. Mrs de Luca commented, 'You certainly put him in his place, Pamela.'

'I realise Italians have quite a lot of name-calling, too. It's the same with us; 'whingeing Poms', some people say. It seems to me that some Aussies don't like anyone who wasn't born here. I just thought that a fellow Brit would be a bit kinder.'

'You're right about prejudice, Pamela. But it's the same between Australians. I hear them calling names; Sydney people saying that Melbourne's Yarra River, she run upside down because she so muddy. And people from Melbourne calling our Harbour Bridge 'The Coat Hanger'.'

It was true. Prejudice was everywhere; even Dave, my boss at work, wasn't shy of making disparaging comments about women.

Arriving at Town Hall Station, we were in the heart of Sydney, close to the big department stores like Anthony Hordern's and Mark Foy's. It was frantic on the crowded streets. With high-rise buildings that towered above us, the streets were in virtual perpetual shadow.

We went into Anthony Hordern's massive store. The last time Sharon and I had been there was just before the previous Christmas. Hard to believe how much she grown since then.

As a treat for Sharon, we visited the toy department. I was conscious that we wouldn't be buying any large items as they would have to be shipped back to England.

Last Christmas, Santa had been here, resplendent in his red suit. Luckily it had been relatively cool in the store.

There had been a special treat for children called Santa's Submarine. Whoever thought that made any logical sense? It was hardly Christmassy. Nevertheless I'd bought tickets and we'd made our way down a sloping passage until we were seated in a narrow tube-shaped room.

After announcements by the so-called

captain that we were submerging to sail under the ocean, bubbles and flowing water had appeared outside the 'portholes'. Then we'd marvelled as brightly coloured fish, sharks, huge whales and starfish on coral reefs passed by our little vessel. Although it had been very cartoony, it had been an absolute treat for the children who'd loved the adventure.

A Christmas submarine for last year? I wondered about this coming year. Asking the manager of the toy department, he confessed that they had no plans as the store was reducing expenditure in all departments, actually laying off staff.

Lots of kiddies would be so disappointed. Maybe the shopping centres could fill the gap.

An idea began to form in my mind. It would be a project for my company, which was in the process of extending one of Sydney's first shopping centres, Waratah World. It was named after the spectacular, bright red flower that was a symbol of New South Wales.

Twelve o'clock came all too soon. Every large shop closed. Sydney quickly emptied of people apart from cinema goers. It almost felt like a ghost town — a shadow of its former self.

Mrs de Luca returned home while Sharon and stayed in town. We had lunch at one of the new Italian restaurants. When I first arrived in Australia there were Chinese restaurants . . . and more Chinese restaurants. Oh, and milk bars that sold fish and chips along with burgers.

After lunch, we went to Hyde Park in the centre of Sydney. It was an oasis in between the sprawling shops, offices and the museum.

I'd only been into Sydney four times in the two years since we'd immigrated. I felt guilty about that, considering we only lived a few miles away. The fact was, I'd not seen much outside of the Western Suburbs where we lived and I worked.

Finding Mrs de Luca had been one

of those lovely touches of Kismet. After the split with Frank, I'd been so depressed. Even if I had the money back then for the return trip to England, I couldn't have afforded to pay back the Australian government for bringing us out here on the ten-pound immigration scheme.

Sharon looked around in delight. She hadn't been in the park before.

'It's like a really big garden, Mummy, with flowers and trees and a water thing.'

I ruffled Sharon's hair, much to her annoyance.

'That water thing is called a fountain. Let's go to have a closer look,' I said to her.

She was fascinated by the Archibald fountain with its statues and jets of water. Then she noticed an ice cream vendor. That was the end of her interest in the fountain.

Later, we sat on the grass. In deference to potentially outraged passers-by, I removed my cardigan and covered my legs before we both lay back. The lawns were lush and dry, with that evocative scent of freshly cut grass enveloping me like a familiar cosy blanket. Closing my eyes, I ran my fingers slowly and sensually through the velvety soft green.

My mind was drawn back through the years. More cool grass touching my bare arms and legs . . . Anglesey . . . a caravan overlooking a beach far below . . . the shrill cries of seagulls overhead with gentle, rhythmic sound of waves lapping the sea shore. Simpler times . . . happier times.

Sharon nudged me. Opening my eyes again, I took her hand to kiss it.

'When I was a little bit older than you, my sister and I used to lie on the grass and look for shapes in the clouds. Shall we try that?' I suggested.

'Mummy. We can't. There aren't any clouds.'

She was correct. Azure blue sky was everywhere. *Another blinking perfect day in paradise*, I thought, disappointed that the moment had been lost.

Then Sharon sat up, staring at the sky to our right. 'What's that?' She pointed.

'It's a plane, darling. Wait . . . What's it doing?'

A trail of white smoke appeared behind the aircraft as it flew in a straight line, then curved gradually until a shape began to form.

'It's sign-writing . . . in the sky,' I realised, smiling. I'd never seen it before. It was a magical first experience we could share. 'What's it saying, Sharon? You know your alphabet. You tell me.'

We watched as over the next fifteen or so minutes it spelled out *Aeroplane Jelly*, a well-known dessert on sale throughout Australia.

Once she realised, Sharon decided to sing the advertisement we'd heard so often on the radio.

'*I like Aeroplane Jelly. Aeroplane Jelly for me.*

I like it for dinner, I like it for tea,

A little each day is a good recipe,
The quality's high, as the name will imply . . . '

Other people in the park heard, and some surprisingly joined in. The song had apparently been around since before I was born and was part of the Aussie tradition that was struggling to emerge. I found myself singing too — more for my daughter's sake than mine. Even so, it felt good to engage with these total strangers.

★   ★   ★

That night, as usual, I made certain that I'd left the dresser lamp lit with the bedroom door open. With the curtains drawn, it would have been far too dark for me. Turning back the sheets, I climbed into my bed and put my glasses on the bedside table.

A rustling sound made me tense momentarily.

'Only scaredy-cats are afraid of the dark,' I recalled my sister teasing once, before Dad had told her off very sternly. He and Mum had seemed to understand my fear, even feeling guilty for it.

I looked up the name of my condition in the school's copy of an encyclopaedia. It was called nyctophobia, from some Latin or Greek words.

Knowing it had a name helped me accept that I wasn't alone. I always associated loneliness with darkness, although I was conscious that I didn't like to get too close to people either. Dad often called me his very own packet of Smarties because there were so many different sides of me all crammed into one little girl. I missed him and Mum a lot.

Sharon was breathing slowly in her bed, fast asleep. I hoped that she was having sweet dreams. My eyes closed

'Not long till I see you both once more,' I whispered, lying back. It had been a long day.

★   ★   ★

A noise woke me with a start. My heart was pounding. Something was wrong. Why was the light out? Why couldn't I hear Sharon's breathing?

I fumbled to find my glasses but knocked them onto the floor. 'Sharon . . . Sharon . . . wake up.'

My mouth was dry. I struggled to breathe. I couldn't hear Sharon at all. It didn't make any sense. Where was the light? I fell out of bed, my feet tangled in the sheets and blankets. Desperately, my hands searched.

She wasn't there. My daughter was gone.

2

This time, I screamed out Sharon's name. There was a noise from the lounge area, although I was so panic-stricken I couldn't make it out. Every part of my body was convulsing as I struggled to make sense of it all.

The door creaked. Someone was there, on the other side. It opened slowly, flooding the bedroom with light. Now a different type of fear engulfed my body. Fear of the blackness made way for dread of whoever was there.

As bravely as I could I demanded, 'Show yourself.'

A silhouette of a figure appeared. Was the intruder that person who had been breaking into houses in the area? If so, he was in for a fight.

'Mu . . . Mummy?' As my eyes adjusted to the light I could see Sharon sobbing. She had a glass in her hand.

Hell. She was shaking. My little girl was scared.

Of me? There was no one else. I'd over-reacted.

'Mummy. What did I do? I was getting water.'

I felt the tension drain from my body. Sharon was OK. However I was angry.

'Sharon. Never, ever close that door at night. I hate being in the dark. You know that.'

I heard her sobbing.

'I'm sorry, Mummy. I forgetted.'

Quickly, I gathered her in my arms, consumed with guilt at my brainless over-reaction.

'Mummy's bad for yelling,' I said soothingly, kissing her head over and over. It was so difficult for me to explain why I felt the way I did about the darkness. After all, children were meant to feel safe with their mother. I hated that Sharon witnessed me being scared of something that was so trivial to everyone else.

It took some time until we were both

asleep again. I actually forced myself to stay awake until her own steady breathing had slowed and I understood she was in her dreams once more.

Of all the things to be afraid of in Sydney, like spiders and snakes and insects, I had to deal with darkness as well. Some useless role model I was.

★   ★   ★

Sunday morning was awkward for me. I'd shown a side of myself to Sharon that I preferred to keep hidden. Worse, that paranoid fear of mine wasn't going away. If anything, it was becoming worse with every terrifying episode I experienced.

Nevertheless I was surprised by Sharon's resilience and maturity. She didn't mention the previous night apart from asking if I was all right.

After breakfast, she went to play in the garden between our flat and Mrs de Luca's home. One thing to be said for Australian gardens, they were unusually large compared to those at home.

I was having a day out on my own — one I'd been talked into by my friend at work, Brenda. She was a sort of secretary cum trouble-shooter to the big chief of our firm and had insisted that I come, in her words, 'to help keep my sanity'. She maintained I was the only person she could relate to at work. There weren't many women in the company, and the majority of those were in the typing and accounts departments.

Somehow I'd managed to convince the company to employ me as a designer for the shopping centres they built, giving a woman's perspective on colours and practicalities such as access for strollers and prams.

In some ways it was an insult — though, without me, some guy would be making the decisions and probably making a hash of them in the process.

Brenda was having a barbecue — or barbie as Aussies insisted on calling it.

It was for adults only. I could only imagine that some parents thought they needed to escape from their responsibilities, which made no sense to me at all.

Sharon and I went to the ten o'clock service at our local church before coming back to our flat. Mrs de Luca, her cat and kittens would entertain Sharon while I was there.

I spent some time getting ready, with Sharon watching, speaking about everything and nothing. It was like having a grown-up there as she was very aware of things other children ignored. My girl was maturing far too quickly.

Together we made decisions about what I should wear. Sharon preferred the fuchsia pink blouse I'd bought before she was born, however the collar was frayed a little. So I decided on my favourite jade green blouse with a white skirt that wasn't too short. As it was something special, for me at least, I made a real effort with my hair and make-up.

'You look beautiful, Mummy.'

I kissed her. I'd always prided myself on making an effort, even for work.

It was a single bus ride to Brenda's. Being Sunday, there was almost an hour between buses so I timed it as best I could, not to have to wait too long.

Luckily, it wasn't a hot day. September was a pleasant month with floral displays adorning the gardens. Fragrant scents and splendid colours were a sign that winter was a thing of the past. There was a pot-pourri of European flowers as well as more drought-resistant Australian natives like wattle and bottlebrush. I thought of this as one of Australia's Goldilocks months . . . not too hot, not too cold. In my shopping bag was a cake I'd baked for the occasion.

The five-minute walk from the bus stop to Brenda's home passed a harbourside park. It was a perfect spring day, disturbed only by the sound of the lawnmowers that every man in Sydney seem to use each weekend. I was reminded of that movie, *Invaders From Mars*. The men were placed under mind-control, doing identical things at the same time.

Every house was what I called a bungalow. They were all detached out here in the suburbs about six miles from Sydney city centre, as there had been more space to build.

Brenda greeted me warmly, almost desperately.

'I must admit, I'm not looking forward to this, Brenda. I don't know any of the people here apart from you and obviously you'll be busy.'

Placing my cake offering in her large fridge, I could see and hear a dozen or so guests outside. Brenda's husband, or hubby, was on barbie duty. A cloud of smoke enveloped him.

'What would you like to drink, Pamela? The blokes are having tinnies,' my friend asked.

'A shandy, thanks.'

It wasn't proper for a member of the fairer sex to drink beer — however a shandy, combining beer and lemonade, was quite acceptable.

'Are you sure there's no one here from work?' I inquired, hopefully.

'No. I tolerate them for five days,' said Brenda. 'I'd hardly want them here too. You, my dear Pamela, are the sole exception.' She gave me a hug. 'It's normally us versus the blokes. I honestly don't have a clue how you tolerate that Dave Garrick.'

My boss believed that a woman's place was at home. We'd had words once or twice during the ten months I'd been working there. Moreover, like many Aussie men, he thought he was the Lord's gift to women.

'Come on. I'll introduce you,' said Brenda. 'My mother's here. She's invited one or two people. Mix the group up a bit. Must say you're decked out — put the rest of us women to shame.'

It was clear that I was overdressed compared to the other guests. Most of the women wore lipstick but no other make-up. I wasn't bothered.

Outside the smell of burning meat permeated the atmosphere. Steak and lamb were cheaper here than in in England. Strangely, Australian men liked to put steak between two slices of bread to make a steak 'sarnie'. Adding some 'dead horse' or tomato sauce would strangely enhance the experience.

Considering that Australia was once one of the colonies, I thought it irreverent to ruin a perfectly good language with their horrible contractions and jargon.

Introductions over, I realised I was the only woman there without a partner. Well, I decided, this was going to be fun.

Then a new guy appeared at the back door; a late arrival. He was by himself, it seemed. My initial elation that I might have someone to talk to evaporated as quickly as it had arrived.

Although he was well groomed with a clean-shaven face and neat, chestnut-coloured hair, his dress sense was positively dire. Lime-green trousers, far too short, revealed aqua-coloured socks above tennis shoes. At least his orange and green checked shirt showed some sense of colour co-ordination.

I must have been staring as I noticed him facing me. What was worse was the broad smile that suddenly appeared. He reminded me of a giant preying mantis poised to pounce.

'Oh no,' I whispered. 'He's coming this way.'

It would have been rude to get up and move elsewhere simply to avoid him. Besides, it was too late. I gritted my teeth and pretended to be studying the petals on a nearby rose bush.

'G'day,' the six-foot-tall insect pro-claimed with all the naïvety of a man who didn't realise he wasn't welcome. 'I'm Nick.'

It was a dilemma. Perhaps if I pretended to be deaf, asleep or dead, he'd take the hint and buzz off away somewhere else?

The silence lasted for what seemed

like hours before he again said, 'Hi. I'm — '

'I heard you the first time, Nick. I was just . . . '

'Trying to ignore me? I understand. Most women think I'm a bit of a dag. I guess, I hoped you might be different. Normally, I wouldn't consider talking to somebody as gorgeous as you. When I noticed you staring back . . . No worries. I'll clear off.'

As far as chat-up lines went, being told you're gorgeous was a bit cheesy. Nonetheless, from the mouth of this green young man, I felt it was genuine.

'Wait . . . You can stay, Nick. My name is Pamela. I'll keep my sunglasses on, though. Your clothing is far too bright for me.'

'English, eh? I love your accent. May I sit down next to you? Wouldn't want to be mistaken for some tall grass and be mown down by an errant lawn-mower.' He laughed.

I patted the cushion by my side. His skin was tanned, like most other men and women over here. He had cut himself shaving. A piece of blotting paper was still on his cheek.

I reached over to retrieve it on impulse but he pulled back hastily. I tapped my own cheek. Nick understood and reached up to peel it off.

We sat there in silence, each staring at the grass in front of us. Finally he did speak.

'Pamela, Pamela. There's a groovy song of that name by Wayne Fontana. Came out last year. Do you know it?'

I didn't and told him so, noticing that he taken off his own sunglasses. His soft, green eyes were so intense, I felt obliged to speak.

'Has anyone ever commented on those eyes of yours, Nick?'

'Only that I have two of them. I think it was my sister when she was a toddler. Why? Going to criticise them too?'

It seemed as though it was going to be a long afternoon. Brenda's husband was still cremating the sausages, steaks and — strangely — pineapple while

Brenda busied herself ferrying salads and breads from the kitchen to the plastic-covered table, ensuring they were covered. The flies were probably the most annoying thing in Australia.

I was tempted to offer Brenda my services once again. She'd already declined but it was an escape route from the jolly green giant.

Nick beat me to it. 'I'll check with Stan if he wants a hand with the snags. Sorry, I mean sausages.' Before I could protest, he was up and off leaving me alone again.

Feeling somewhat relieved as well as guilty, I surveyed the other guests. Women were the worst, resenting single females as they protectively held onto their husband's hands.

Men, on the other hand, often wanted to talk to me in group situations where they could hide behind the company of others. I wasn't unattractive, especially with my make-up on. I was tall, blue-eyed, with auburn hair which I normally wore in a long page-boy style similar to Sandie Shaw. I'd been told my voice had a sultry tone which again put me at odds with some women who thought I spoke that way only to attract men. As if. My measurements were close to the 36-28-36 inch hourglass figure that men appeared to like but which again, I had little control over.

Looks aside, I wasn't some dumb brunette who treated her man as a demi-god. I spoke my mind, something most men disliked, branding me awkward or abrasive. Maybe that was why Frank had chosen to desert me . . . that and a ten-year age gap with his new girlfriend.

I tried to present myself well, not for the males of the world, but for me. I hadn't stayed at school past fifteen although I did realise I was smart. My confidence suffered a bit when Frank had run off, but that was his choice. My little girl and I were all the better in retrospect — though losing anyone you love always hurts at the time.

One of the ladies disappeared inside, presumably to the loo. Immediately her husband began moving my way. His stomach arrived five seconds before the rest of him.

'Hi, little lady. You look lonely over here. Reckon you could do with a real man to brighten up your day.' He stank of cigarettes.

I looked up at him, then craned my neck.

'Where is he?' I asked.

'Who?' he replied, appearing totally puzzled.

'This real man you mentioned.'

His smile changed in an instant as he scowled at me. He was wearing that greasy Brylcreem hair cream. In spite of it being obvious that he hadn't shaved. I could smell Californian Poppy. He was a dinosaur from the fifties for sure.

Then he moved closer, towering over me intimidatingly. Once again my big mouth had landed me in trouble.

'I don't like stuck-up sheilas who talk

back. Women should be seen and not heard.'

It was clear he wasn't leaving. Then I heard a familiar voice.

'Sorry I was so long getting your drink, Pammy. Has this bloke been keeping you company?'

Nick handed me another shandy. My hands were shaking a little as I grasped it and downed half the glass. Although taller, Nick would be no match for beer-belly man if it came to blows.

'Is this sheila yours?' he asked Nick, eyeing his green clothing collection warily.

'Yeah, mate. Practically engaged,' was Nick's cheery reply. I could see he was sweating, and it wasn't from the afternoon sun.

'Apologies, sport. Thought she was on her Pat Malone. No hard feelings?'

He extended a huge hand. Nick shook it, only wincing from the pain after the big guy had left us.

It was a good thing my recent admirer hadn't noticed the almost full glass of shandy on the path by my side.

'Thanks, Nick. I have a tendency to get into what you Aussies call a bit of strife. One thing, though — never, ever call me Pam or Pammy again. Do you understand, Nickykins?'

He grinned. 'Yeah. Sure thing.'

'We'll forget about the practically engaged bit also, thank you. You're far too young for me.'

'If you don't mind me asking, how old are you?'

'Twenty-nine.' Unlike a lot of women, I wasn't offended when a guy asked my age.

'I'm twenty-six. Not much younger,' he protested. 'I simply have a baby face.'

If he were twenty-six, he was correct about his complexion. He still had signs of acne.

'Tell me, Mr Knight-in-shiny-green-armour. What is it that you do with yourself?'

He took a drink of some dark liquid.

'I'm a teacher. All white shirts and

dark trousers in the week which is why I like to splash out on colour during my weekends. Have a blast.'

'At least you have white tennis shoes,' I observed.

'Only because they don't do green. Perhaps one day they will. That'd be unreal.'

'What about your spare time?' I was intrigued. Teachers normally had to be self confident and assertive. This man seemed to be pretending to be like that yet I sensed underneath he was unsure. His over-use of trendy vernacular seemed quite put on. Maybe I was being too judgmental.

Nick hesitated. 'I'm in a church choir. We've started practising our Christmas carols already. Apart from that, nothing much. I live at home with my parents not far from here.'

That surprised me. 'I thought you would be too old to be with your parents.'

He paused again, staring at his open hands.

'I was divorced last year. She wanted more from life. Guess that's why women don't want to go out with me. I'm second-hand goods.'

He'd opened up to me, which was more than men usually did.

'I'm also divorced,' I confided. 'Actually, I have a daughter.'

I felt a connection to him. Men treated me as second-hand as well, often expecting me to be more ... *accommodating* than a single woman. They ended up being quite disappointed.

I was old-fashioned like that. The Britain I'd left had begun to be more permissive in recent years. The use of the Pill and pop stars' life styles had brought about changes in relationships, not all of them good.

'What's your little girl's name?' He appeared interested.

'Sharon.' I opened my purse. 'I have her photograph.' Showing him the coloured picture, I added, 'She's four years old.'

Nick took the photo and examined it. 'She's fab, just like her mother.'

'Fab?' I laughed in spite of myself. 'You do realise that not many people are comfortable using that word any longer?'

'I still use it. I learnt it from the British magazine called *Fabulous* back in 1963. I used to read it on the train home from school. Back then I was in love with Dusty Springfield.' There was a hesitation in his voice when he added, 'Er . . . My first post as a teacher.'

On cue, there was the sound of a school bell being rung vigorously.

'Tucker's all ready, folks. Grab a plate and help yourselves,' Brenda announced.

Nick and I remained seated as the others crowded around the table. There were chairs from the kitchen plus folding chairs. People struggled to balance the paper plates of food while they sat down to eat, the occasional snag falling to the lawn where Brenda's daschund disposed of it immediately.

Nick must have been watching too.

''Spose that's why they call them sausage dogs,' he joked.

I laughed. It was actually funny.

Eventually we wandered over together and returned, pleased that our seats hadn't been occupied in our absence.

To me, there was a lot of blackness on our plates. The meat hadn't been so much cooked as incinerated. Nick explained that the charcoal added to the flavour. I wasn't convinced.

The salad was much better. Beetroot seem to be a favourite vegetable for Australians, coming straight out of the tin. I put two serviettes on my top and another on my lap. My blouse was more like a shirt with a collar and buttons down the front. The top button had become undone although I hadn't realised.

'Try the pineapple,' Nick suggested.

It was surprisingly full of flavour. Over here there was an abundance of fruit — some of which, like mango and pawpaw, I hadn't heard of before. I remembered, I was a teenager before I had my first banana due to the rationing after the war.

We found a lot to discuss. At some times he appeared very shy, at others unusually gregarious.

Who was the real Nick? I found myself wondering. Why was I even bothered? I'd never see him again after today. He was simply a distraction, albeit a strangely pleasant one.

He confessed to reading comics. I was shocked. After all, he was an educated grown man.

'What? Like Mickey Mouse?'

He chuckled. 'Not quite. Superheroes like Batman and Green Lantern. Donovan mentioned Green Lantern in his song *Sunshine Superman*.' Even though I wasn't into pop music, I had heard that song a lot. Nick wasn't finished with his bizarre revelations. 'I even draw my own, too. I use them in class sometimes.'

I understood now that I was talking

to the biggest kid I'd ever met. In a way, it was liberating.

'That's interesting, Mr Nick Winters. Answer me a question, please. If I were a super-heroine, what would I be called?'

He mused on that for a moment before replying. 'Sarcastic Lass.'

I bristled a little inside at being perceived that way, but I could live with it. Better than Welcome-Mat Woman who'd let men walk all over her.

I noticed him looking at me from head to toe.

'Don't tell me. You're imagining me in some skin-tight brightly coloured costume.'

He blushed. My joke wasn't a joke at all.

'I'm disappointed, Nick. Just when I think you're a halfway decent man, you say or do something stupid. No wonder your wife left you.'

I regretted the last statement the moment I'd said it. I could hardly cast the first stone.

To his credit, he didn't throw my own divorce back in my face.

'Sorry, Nick. I guess Sarcastic Lass has struck again.' I put a hand on his, smiling.

He grinned back before pointing to my chest.

I looked down. Some tomato on my blouse had sneaked past the serviettes. At least, I hoped it was tomato. Beetroot would be a big problem.

'Excuse me,' I said, putting my plate to one side and taking my handbag. Desserts, including my own cake, had just been brought outside.

I collared Brenda, indicating the stain.

'Where's the bathroom, please?'

'I'll show you, Pamela,' she said. We went inside as she added, 'That bloke and you seem to be doing OK. Quite a hunk. What's his name?'

'Nick. Isn't he a friend of yours?'

'No. Obviously he fancies you. Reckon he's a bit young, though. He works at the school where my mum is a secretary. She invited him.'

In the bathroom, I took my glasses from my bag, wondering if I should remove my contacts then use the glasses to see the stain better. The light wasn't very good. In the end, I decided against it. The stain came out fine.

Returning outside, I grabbed some cake — I suspected mine was the only one made from scratch. The others screamed White Wings cake mix packets — which were OK, but not proper baking like my mum taught me.

Nick was already tucking into his third piece.

'This one's best,' he announced.

'I made that. Banana cake with fresh bananas.'

Some of the crowd began to say their goodbyes soon after. I realised how late it was and that my eyes were beginning to hurt. The bright Australian sunshine took some getting used to, even though I wore sunglasses most of the time outside.

'Nick. I need to leave now. It's been a

pleasure meeting you,' I said, standing to shake his hand. He got up also.

'Pamela, I was wondering if you could . . . maybe . . . well, go out with me, next weekend?'

'You and me? Like on a date? I don't think so.'

The expression on his face reminded me of Sharon when I refused her a request for an ice cream. I felt compelled to add an explanation, if only to lessen his sad-puppy-dog look.

'I'm moving back to the UK within three months. It will be permanent. I plan to spend this Christmas there with my family. Quite frankly, it's unthinkable for me to begin any sort of relationship with a man, no matter who they are.'

A plane was flying overhead so I raised my voice slightly. 'And if you're thinking of some short-term physical relationship, forget it. I have more respect for my daughter and my own body than to do one-night stands.'

Well. That didn't come out the way

I'd intended, judging from the embarrassed looks from Nick and the three people close enough to hear me.

All the same, Nick had to have the last word.

'You might think this is the final time we'll see one another, Pamela — yet I have the strangest feeling that we'll meet again.'

I left with a quick farewell and thanks to Brenda and her husband. No doubt she'd hear the full story before I saw her at work the next day.

I'd be off the list for future barbecues. Sarcastic Lass had certainly made an impression. I took a clean handkerchief from my bag to dab my eyes.

*   *   *

The bus journey home was uneventful, as was tea with Sharon. My eyes were stinging more and more as we ate, probably from being around the barbecue smoke for all those hours. I needed to remove my contact lenses.

Before I could do so, Sharon commented, 'Why are your eyes so red, Mummy?'

I searched my bag for my glasses. Only then did I remember; I'd left them in Brenda's bathroom. My eyes were feeling much more irritated now, making it hard to even open them. One glimpse in the mirror reminded me of Christopher Lee as a vampire in those Hammer horror films.

Taking the contacts out would leave me unable to see very well at all. What could I do?

3

I had to make some quick decisions. Although I wasn't as blind as the proverbial bat without my glasses or contacts, it would make the evening very difficult for me without them.

I splashed water on my eyes. It helped a bit but I needed to take out the contacts as quickly as possible. Before that, I removed my notebook from my bag and frantically searched for Brenda's phone number.

Sharon would have to read it. Even opening my eyes a little was now becoming too difficult.

Finally, I used the suction cups to remove the contacts, more by touch than sight. Bathing my eyes in water gave me relief at long last.

'Stupid, stupid, stupid,' I muttered. I'd meant to buy a spare pair of glasses for ages but delayed it, telling myself they were an extravagance when money for our flights was the priority.

Sharon was already in her nightie and dressing gown. Grasping her hand, I opened the door.

'Come on, sweetheart,' I told her. 'We're going to the phone box.'

It was late, coming up to dusk. We had no phone or television. Mrs de Luca didn't have a phone either.

Holding the paper with Brenda's phone number as well as some change, we opened the glass panelled door. It took some time because I had to hold Sharon high up to reach the dial, plus her fingers struggled to pull it around each time. At last I was connected.

'Brenda? It's me, Pamela. I need your help.'

'Sure, Pamela. Anything for my new star attraction.' There was a pause. 'You turned our barbie from OK into a real day to remember. Thanks.'

I was shocked. 'Perhaps I should charge by the hour next time. Seriously though, I left my glasses in your bathroom.'

'Found them already. Didn't think you wore specs, though.'

Explaining my predicament, I asked if someone might drop them off. It was too late for the buses.

'Stan's had a skinful and I can't drive. Perhaps that young bloke, Nick? He's about to leave.'

It seemed like no glasses then. Damn.

I explained, 'He was drinking too.'

'Only Pepsi,' Brenda replied. 'He has a car and apparently you're on the way home.'

It was a relief. Then I realised.

'Brenda. He doesn't know where I live.'

My friend's answer made me smile.

'Nick said it doesn't matter. Even if there's a detour, you're on the way home.'

Sharon had done a brilliant job, helping me. She guided me home to wait. There was no guarantee that I could wear my contacts tomorrow morning if the swelling didn't subside.

Nick arrived within ten minutes. I heard him enter by the squeaky side gate.

Opening our front door, I almost grabbed my glasses to put them on. The vague figure in the doorway was instantly transformed into a clear image of Nick . . . green clothing included.

'Who's this young lady?' he inquired, kneeling down. Sharon hid behind my skirt, peeking out.

'Say hello, Sharon. This is Nick. He's . . . a friend of Mummy's.'

'Hello, Mr Nick,' she said, timidly.

'Like to come in?' It was the least I could do.

The room was about fifteen feet square with a comfy old-style settee plus a Formica table and chairs. I indicated the settee while I sat on a dining chair with Sharon on my lap. I was conscious that he was appraising our home.

'It's small but it suits us,' I explained,

a little self-consciously.

He grinned back. 'Actually it's fab. When I get back on my feet, I'll find somewhere of my own again. Just not yet.'

'Thanks for bringing me these.' I tapped my frames. 'The smoke must have irritated my eyes. I was wearing contacts and . . . '

'You don't need to explain, Pamela. Only too pleased to assist a damsel in distress. Chivalry is what us knights do. It's in our job description.'

I recalled my earlier comment when Nick saved me from Brylcreem Man.

Nick struggled to push himself up from the settee. Some of the springs had gone.

'If that's all, I'd best get on my way. I need to prepare a lesson for tomorrow.'

'Oh yes, you're a teacher. What do you teach?'

'Normally I'd come back with a comment like 'teenage horrors' but that's not true. I love my job. I teach French.'

Despite my sore eyes, I was impressed and showed it. 'How wonderful. Say something please.' I caught sight of a wicked gleam in those green eyes of his.

'Je t'adore, mon petit chou-fleur. It means, 'I like you, my friend'.'

'Actually it means, 'I adore you, my little cauliflower',' I observed to Nick's obvious embarrassment. The French had a peculiar interest in being affectionate to vegetables.

'You speak French?'

'Bah oui. Comme une vache espagnole.' My accent wasn't great so I admitted I spoke like a Spanish cow, a common expression in Paris. My year in France had been a steep learning curve.

'As I said, I must be off, Pamela and Sharon.'

He reached the door before I caught up with him. Placing my hand on his to stop him opening it, I reminded him that he he'd predicted we'd meet again as I'd left the barbie.

'Are you always that certain about the future, Nick?'

He laughed, turning his face from mine.

'Far from it. Each day after I broke up from my wife, I've struggled, especially with school. Why do you think I moved back home? Even thought about giving up my job. It's not easy when you're depressed. Tried drinking to dull the pain. That didn't work at all. I'm one of those very un-Aussie blokes who can't deal with alcohol . . . some enzyme deficiency. Can you believe that? I'm a failure, exactly as my ex-wife told me.'

'Hence you drinking Pepsi at the party. If it helps, I understand what break-ups and divorce do to a person. Without Sharon, I don't know how I would have coped. And, like you, I can't drink spirits. A shandy or one wine. Any more and I'm . . . ' I stopped, conscious of Sharon listening.

Putting my other hand on his also, I thought I could feel his pulse increase as my fingers grasped his wrist. 'That offer to go out next weekend . . . is it still available?'

Nick met my gaze with that engaging, boyish, enthusiastic smile.

'As a friend, of course?' I added.

'Naturally. I was considering the point you mentioned earlier. You're returning to Pommieland . . . sorry, England? The both of you? Yet you've not seen much of Australia from what you've told me. It seems only fair to let you and Sharon at least discover what there is here. For instance, have either of you ever been on an Aussie train or ferry?'

Sharon answered for us.

'We went on a submarine . . . '

'Christmas display in a Sydney store last year,' I explained. 'Sharon loved it. I think she'll enjoy a train and ferry as well.'

It sounded interesting. Sadly I'd never seen the Harbour Bridge for real, or that strange-looking Opera House they were building.

'Saturday OK?'

'I'm busy on Saturdays, I'm afraid. Sunday? After church, at eleven suit you?'

It did. 'We can have a picnic basket in the Botanical Gardens,' Nick suggested. 'I can organise that.'

'No. Let us. It's the least we can do. Any requests?'

'Anything for me, Pamela. Apart from egg. Er . . . I have a problem with the smell . . . a childhood phobia I haven't gotten over. No quiche, omelettes either, but cakes are fine. Don't ask . . . '

I recalled my own problem with those mothballs and said nothing.

He leaned over to whisper in my ear.

'No funny business, I promise.'

My hands were still on his. I took them off and moved away, hugging Sharon to my leg as he opened the door.

'Not very fair on you, Nick.'

'I'm thinking of it as practice for when I meet a proper future girlfriend.'

With that he left. No kiss goodbye; not even a handshake. Nevertheless, I'd set the ground rules about our relationship. A small part of me regretted that. He appeared to be a caring, considerate man and, in my experience, there were far too few of them around.

* * *

The following morning I dropped Sharon off at the local kindergarten. She loved going there. Mrs de Luca collected her at three and cared for her until I returned home at five-thirty.

The whites of my eyes had calmed down to a baby pink colour, good enough to chance the contacts again after their nightly cleaning.

Waratah World was simply a fifteen minute bus ride from Sharon's 'school'. Being there earlier than Dave allowed me to check on progress of the massive extension to the two-storey undercover complex. Protection from the harsh Aussie sun plus innovative air conditioning was attracting more and more family shoppers.

We had to wear hard hats on the site. Also I usually wore a white coverall over my slacks and blouse as dust was all around.

'You're early, Pamela,' Dave said when he arrived, wearing his own protection.

'I had an idea for Christmas, boss.' The distant sound of jack-hammers and riveting guns reminded us this was a major work in progress. 'Come on and I'll explain.'

There was a temporary barrier across an area of about nine hundred square yards and the back wall of the existing centre ground floor. It had been finished as far as being a large, empty space ready for a department store to begin trading in March. As such, it could easily be closed off from the continued building works and accessed from the original centre walkways.

'Why not set up a Christmas

attraction in here temporarily? Management want one to boost numbers of visitors, and this space is ideal.'

Dave surveyed the huge empty area. Our voices echoed everywhere.

'Too big for a Santa's Grotto, Pamela.'

He sounded quite negative but I had a bold vision, far beyond the conventional set-up.

'Remember that miniature train and track we have in storage after dismantling that amusement park?' He nodded. 'How about setting it up as Santa's Train, going through a winding tunnel to the grotto? On the way it would pass dioramas of scenes around the North Pole, giving passengers a real feeling that they've travelled there.'

He stroked his chin. 'Four carriages, ten seats a carriage. A bit of paintwork, an elf driving it . . . any ideas on the dioramas?'

'I'm thinking a token admission to help cover costs, plus photos in the grotto and on the train? We have enough mannequins, plus Christmas displays in storage. There's a plastic reindeer stowed down there, I just checked the inventory. We could put it in a field with painted fir trees and other reindeer. Maybe have his nose light up?'

'Like . . . what's his name? Blitzen?'

'Ruldolph, actually.'

Dave was becoming engaged. 'The budget?' I told him.

'It's a lot for a temporary exhibit. I can't see it being feasible.'

'We can run it for five weeks from mid November.' I thought it was a viable time frame to build it. That many days would give the news about it time to spread via word of mouth plus allowing for repeat visits.

'Tell you what, Pamela. Type that proposal of yours up. Include some sketches of dioramas. I'll let HJ know and we'll see what he reckons. He'll liaise with centre management. Fair enough?'

I felt better after that. I usually got on

with Dave, in spite of the occasional sexual innuendo and disparaging comment about women in general.

HJ was the one who'd chosen to employ me over all of those male candidates. At least now I'd contribute something positive during my final few months of service with the firm.

I did as Dave suggested, giving him a typed proposal with carbons to pass on to HJ the following morning.

★   ★   ★

Tuesday lunchtime saw HJ arrive on site. He appeared excited.

'Pamela. Have you heard about this idea of Dave's? Santa's Train? It's inspired.'

'Idea of Dave's . . . ?' I began before my boss interrupted.

'Pamela knows all about it, HJ. She typed it up after I explained it. She's done some fine sketches of my ideas, too.' Dave glared at me from behind HJ's back. I recognised that expression from far too many men. It was the look of *Shut your mouth, girlie, if you know what's good for you.*

HJ had obviously been duped . . . and so had I.

HJ wasn't finished. 'Well done, Dave. An exceptional plan. Progressive thinking. It's what I like to see in my managers. I've OKed your plans and budget. You can get moving on it right away.'

After that demoralising incident, I hid myself away for the rest of the day. If Dave was taking the credit, he could blinking well do all the work also. How could he do this to me?

The simple answer was that he could and he did. I was a woman and he was my boss. So much for the women's equality movement I'd read had started overseas. What was it that George Orwell had written in his book *Animal Farm*?

We're all created equal but some are more equal than others.

Worse still, Dave found me and made

it abundantly clear what I should do and that I had no choice whatsoever. He then magnanimously dumped all of the project's practicalities on my lap, leaving me in our joint temporary office to get on with it.

I was furious. What could I do? I needed the job for saving the remaining money I required for the plane fares, so it was sort of one of those Catch-22 situations where I couldn't win, no matter what I did.

Before I left that evening, I took one photo of a smiling Dave from a few pinned to his cork-board and scrunched it up into my handbag. It was a petty thing to do, yet at least it was something. Pity I didn't have a dartboard at home.

* * *

At home, I took great joy in cutting the picture into increasingly small pieces. It made me feel a little better though I understood that a man had hurt me

72

once more. I decided then and there, *never again*.

As I prepared dinner, I asked Sharon about her day, taking pains to gently correct her English as she spoke. She was a quick learner, even surprising me by uttering 'Bah oui,' when I asked if she wanted baked beans with the sausages.

'You do know what 'oui' means, sweetheart?'

'Yes. It's like 'si' in Italian. It means, 'yes'.'

That was a revelation. 'You're learning Italian from Mrs de Luca?'

'Si, mama mia,' she responded with a giggle.

I gave her a huge hug and kiss. It was a pity that I'd noticed that a few insipid Australianisms were sneaking into her vocabulary also. I wondered where she'd been learning them. Then I recalled her telling me about that new Australian television show about some kangaroo or wallaby. She watched it at Mrs de Luca's; *Jumpy* or something.

Sharon went on to inform me of the latest escapades of Mrs de Luca's cat and her babies, asking if she could have one of the kittens when they were old enough.

I tried to explain that it would be unfair to the kitten to become her pet when she would have to say goodbye in a few months.

'We're leaving here before Christmas, sweetheart. You know that.'

'How many sleeps is that, Mummy?'

I did a quick calculation and held up both hands a number of times.

'Goodness, Mummy. That's an awfully lot of sleeps. I'll be a growed-up woman by then.'

I gritted my teeth despite smiling at her childish logic. Sharon was imitating one of the women from the kindy. She used 'awfully' an awful lot.

Then I mentally kicked myself. 'Kindy' instead of kindergarten? I was becoming contaminated myself. Arrghh! The sooner we both escaped this mixed-up country, the better.

Once Sharon was in bed, I settled down on the lumpy settee to re-read those latest aerogrammes. Mum and my sister were keen to see Sharon yet there was no mention of me. Was I being paranoid? After all, we hadn't been that close since I'd left home six years earlier to travel to the continent.

Lorraine had her own family and lived quite a distance from my parents. Was I being a dreamer to expect to be a prodigal daughter, returning home to open arms and an idyllic life in the Manchester cold and rain? I honestly wasn't sure.

★   ★   ★

During the following three days, I hardly saw Dave. Although it was my choice to begin with, I think he took the hint fairly quickly. He did ask about a missing photo. I suggested that one of the female staff may have taken it to place under her pillow. The next time I saw him he was making a pest of himself in the staff dining room, offering signed photos to any woman who wanted one.

Doing the bare minimum of work on 'Dave's Santa Train' project had been an option early on. Nevertheless that part of me that strove to do my best at work took over. Besides, it was for the kiddies; a Christmas treat. At least when I brought Sharon for a ride once it was finished, we'd both know whose idea it was.

Brenda came in every day for a progress report. The diorama designs included Santa's workshop (naturally), the reindeer grazing and playing, Mrs Claus reading letters by the fireside in their cosy home and finally the grotto with Santa, some elves and the sleigh stacked with presents.

Yet I wanted something else; something to make Santa's Train Ride an experience to make the children and adults gasp with wonder and joy.

The construction team had already fabricated the winding tunnel and offset 'caves' for the displays the train would pass. The train, carriages and track were due to arrive in late October.

Outside of the building zone, Waratah World was already advertising the upcoming Christmas spectacle and had chosen to include it in the pre-Christmas television advertising.

I was proud of what I was achieving. Sadly I was angry at what Dave had done. It was a difficult week. When Friday evening came, I was actually looking forward to the weekend and seeing Nick. A trip to Sydney Harbour? Peace, fun and a lovely day out with Sharon away from any drama.

How wrong could I have been?

* * *

Sunday morning saw Nick arrive precisely on time. He was dressed much more conservatively which was a welcome surprise. His car was a Holden, the brand that Australian men seemed to regard as a symbol of their country. It was a few years old, grey and white. It also didn't appear to have been washed in all that time.

'I thought all Australian men cleaned their cars once a week,' I commented, gingerly opening the door. At least the inside looked tidy.

'I'm not like other men, Miss Pamela. Thought you would have realised that by now.'

'At least any future girlfriend of yours will have the added benefit of a good acre of topsoil available for her garden,' I muttered under my breath. If he heard me, he said nothing.

There was space for three on the front bench seat; however Nick insisted that Sharon sat in the back. Strangely, he had a special child seat belt there for her, as well as two belts in the front. I doubted they were a recent purchase.

'Did you and your ex have any children, Nick?'

'Kids? No, we didn't. Why do you ask?'

'No reason.' It was none of my

business, I decided. At least he was safety-conscious. New South Wales was talking about making seat belts compulsory but no law had been passed as yet.

Sharon was a little apprehensive as we'd not really travelled in cars, apart from the occasional taxi. I didn't drive. Perhaps I'd learn back in Britain but, like televisions and telephones, driving lessons were an extravagance I couldn't afford. Savings for our flights home were the priority. Another month and I'd see the travel agent.

Nick drove us to Croydon station where we purchased tickets for the return train journey. A newly built double-decker train arrived soon afterwards.

'Follow me upstairs,' Nick announced once we had boarded. I was overjoyed to see the look on Sharon's face. On the way into Sydney, she pointed out a neon sign on the side of a smoke-stained building.

'It's another Aeroplane Jelly plane,' she announced to us.

Those houses we could see had roofs of either painted galvanised iron or red tiles. Sydney, like most cities, had railways surrounded by rubbish and overgrown weeds. However the trains were clean and comfortable.

Passing Central Station, the train went underground through a tunnel. *Just like my Santa Train*, I thought.

'We'll get off at Circular Quay,' Nick announced. 'Three more stops.'

That station was a recent extension to the underground and when we alighted, Sharon and I were both spellbound. With the tunnel on either side we were high up, overlooking the harbour.

'Wow,' I said, genuinely impressed. A hundred feet below us was the ferry terminal with ferries going to and fro across the sparkling azure waters. The Harbour Bridge towered above us on the left, taking cars and trains to the northern suburbs. On the right there was building work on the harbourside.

'Is that . . . ?'

'The Opera House. They're still working on the interior. Should all have been finished five years ago.'

We took the escalator down from the raised platform, showed our tickets to the inspector on the gate and walked into the sunshine by the water. Sharon wanted to watch the ferries until Nick reminded her we were going on one later.

'First I'm taking my two English roses into a garden . . . a very special garden.'

We walked towards Bennelong Point and the massive shell of the Opera House, then climbed some stairs to one of the most breathtaking views I'd ever experienced. On the water there were dozens of leisure craft and yachts scurrying around like ants on a summer day. Nick pointed out the Oriana as she sailed in from the ocean, probably bringing another boatload of immigrants like us. All around us there were mature trees of every variety, natives as well as those from other parts of the world. The scents of thousands of flowers wafted past us as we explored, eventually sitting down at a table.

'Not a bad view,' I commented, tongue-in-cheek while arranging our picnic feast. We ate under a Jacaranda tree, its branches clothed in light purple blossom with a sweet honey smell. Every now and then, one would fall to the grass, like lilac snowflakes in the late September breeze.

Nick quickly befriended Sharon, including her in our conversations and listening to her attentively. In some ways he seemed like a child himself rather than a mature bloke. Moreover Sharon absolutely loved his dreadful jokes.

Sharon became so relaxed, she decided to share a point that was clearly on her mind. It was something I would have thought she'd ask me, yet she chose him instead. I was surprised.

'Terry Nolan calls me a Pom because I was born in England. What does that mean, Nick?'

It was a word I wasn't comfortable with. Perhaps Sharon had sensed that.

'When people first came to Australia from England, it was a long journey on boats and many of them became sick from not eating fruit every day. Therefore someone very clever decided to give them a type of fruit called a pomegranate which is sort of like an orange. Eventually Australians would see English people arriving here with pomegranates so they started calling them Poms. Do you understand?'

'Then it's not a bad word, like ones that Mummy uses sometimes when she's angry. Words like 'damn' and — '

'I think Nick gets the idea, Sharon,' I said quickly. 'Why don't you play a bit? Don't go far.'

Once she ran a little way off to gambol with some butterflies, I had to explain.

'I don't like the word myself but I guess it's who uses it and how. Also I thought 'Pom' was an acronym for Prisoner of Mother England that the convicts wore on their shirts.'

Nick shrugged. 'Who knows? I've heard that too but my vitamin C theory has one bit of compelling evidence. Before Australia, England sent convicts to America until the 1776 revolution.'

'Yeah. That's true. But Yanks don't call English people Pommies. They call them Limeys.'

Nick grinned. 'Limeys? From . . . ?'

Then I realised. 'From eating limes.' They also had vitamin C. 'You're a clever man, Mr Winters. You're right about that word, Pommies . . . maybe. I guess you're never too old to learn.'

We gathered our belongings to leave.

'Are we really going on a ship, Nick?' Sharon asked as we walked back to the ferry terminal.

'You bet, pumpkin.'

Sharon was enthralled as we embarked and set off across the waves. The smell of the salt spray was invigorating. Even though I wished I'd brought a camera, my old Box Brownie would have been too bulky.

Nick produced a compact camera from his pocket and, to our delight, snapped a number of photos of us with Sydney's landmarks in the background. An older lady kindly offered to take one of the three of us with Sharon in the middle.

'What a lovely family you have,' she said to Nick as she handed the camera back.

Neither Nick nor I contradicted her. There didn't seem much point to a stranger. In addition, it felt good to be thought of as a family rather than receiving pity for being divorced. Many people regarded that as a sign of failure.

'Is the film black and white?' I asked him.

'Colour. They cost more to develop but I prefer them. I'll get an extra set for you.'

'Thanks,' I said, feeling a little guilty that he kept insisting on paying for everything, in spite of my objections.

Disembarking, we had to cross a wide plank. I was anticipating visiting

Manly Beach with the huge Morton Bay Fig trees along the boulevard that Nick had described on the ferry. As we made our way to the undercover terminal exit, there was a commotion behind us. Some woman was shouting for help. We all glanced back. It took a moment to focus on the cause.

'It's the lady who took our photo,' I said, recognising her striped dress. She was collapsed on the ground near the gangplank. A younger woman was kneeling by her side. She was frantic.

'Help us. It's my mum. I can't feel her pulse.'

4

No one moved. There was no sound either. The woman cried out again.

'Please. She needs a doctor. Now.'

I felt so helpless. All of these people, yet not one was able to help. One man called out that he was going to find a phone. By the time an ambulance would arrive, it'd be too late.

'Nick — ' I said, only to find he'd gone. When I turned back to the collapsed woman, Nick was kneeling by her side.

'Move back,' he ordered the crowd. As one, they shuffled back to give him more room. The woman's daughter was crying hysterically. Nick felt the woman's wrist, then her neck before he gently arranged her on the wooden floor.

'I'm starting CPR,' he said to the daughter. 'Loosen her clothing, please, and help me turn her over.'

What followed was so frightening. I protected Sharon as much as I could, bending down to explain as I buried her head in the folds of my dress. What if the woman died despite Nick's attempt to revive her?

He was pushing repeatedly on her chest with the heel of both hands, stopping only to breathe into her mouth every five seconds or so. The younger woman continued to check for a pulse, struggling to contain her tears. The crowd waited expectantly, reverently. It seemed to go on forever. Finally, the daughter wiped her eyes.

'She's breathing,' she stammered, just as two ambulance officers pushed through the ever-expanding group of onlookers.

'Is she . . . ?' someone called out as they took charge. I saw Nick stand, watching them check the woman over quietly and professionally.

Through the moving throng, I caught a glimpse of her. The patient had her eyes open but remained still.

'Think she'll be all right,' one of the uniformed men announced to the assemblage. There was a mixture of cheers and sighs of relief. I told Sharon it was fine. We had to wait for a few minutes until Nick returned.

'The ambos wanted my details. They're taking Gwen to hospital.'

'You saved her life, Nick. You were brilliant,' I told him.

'I teach lifesaving at school. I guess all of that training I did with the surf lifesavers paid off. I was surprised no one else stepped up. Life-saving is taught a lot to the kids here.'

'Maybe people do know what to do theoretically but have second thoughts when they realise that someone's life depends on them doing it right.'

'Maybe. I'm just pleased it worked out.'

'Will you tell your students that you're a real-life superhero?' I asked as we followed the crowd out of the terminal building into the sun.

Nick was aghast. 'Never. My own life is private.'

We walked on towards the promenade of Manly. Somehow seeing the iconic beach front paled into insignificance after the drama we'd been a part of; saving Gwen's life. I began to appreciate how special Nick was.

$$\star \quad \star \quad \star$$

It was after seven when we arrived back home. The day had certainly been one to remember. It was Sharon who asked if we were seeing Nick again. He glanced at me.

'Depends on your Mummy, Sharon. Another day of adventures?'

Sharon showed no ill-effects from the trauma with that woman, Gwen. Nick told me he'd phone the hospital later to check on her situation.

I nodded. 'If it's OK with you, Nick?'

'Let's see . . . I think a surprise day out next weekend. How does that sound?'

Sharon clapped her hands.

'We love surprises, don't we, Mummy?'

'Saturday might be better than Sunday?' I suggested.

'It'll have to be Sunday. Saturdays . . . well, I'm always busy then.'

It was later, after Nick had left, that I wondered what he might be doing. Choir practice was at night. At that point I realised that I was being overly possessive. We weren't any more than companions. Yeah . . . simply friends.

★ ★ ★

Monday morning felt different. The brisk tinge to the air was gone, the warmth of the sun seemed more intense and there was no glistening dew on the grass as we left for Sharon's kindergarten. Also the sunshine was so intense that, without my sunglasses, I'm certain I would have been squinting. It wasn't long after eight o'clock.

European countries like Spain had a siesta during the hottest part of the day.

It made sense to them and to sensible people all over the world . . . apart from Australians, it seemed. Moreover the desire to make Australia a copy of the Mother Country as far as plants and gardens went often saw half-dead roses and camellias quietly wondering what they'd done wrong to be subjected to the heat and drought out here. I'm sure that, if given a choice and a plane ticket they would all uproot themselves to leave on the first flight available. An Aussie summer was the nearest thing to hell I could imagine.

Not that Australians would admit they found it too hot. The perspiration might be pouring off them, and sitting in a car would be like a sauna yet, to them, that was the sign of 'ripper' weather. Oz was the lucky country; sun, sand and surf.

Nick had admitted to me that he used to sunbathe as a teenager, in his back garden.

'I used olive oil,' he confessed. 'I thought it'd give me a decent tan though it usually resulted in peeling skin that hurt for days and left me a patchwork of red and brown splotches.'

Noses were the first to blister. It was the Rudolph effect. It was fashionable to wear white zinc cream to protect them; it was now trendy for sun-bronzed blokes and sheilas.

⋆ ⋆ ⋆

I took the bus to work after dropping Sharon off. Even with the windows open, it wasn't a pleasant experience. Most Australians hadn't discovered deodorant, a necessity in the heat. Men seemed more reluctant to accept them, even the new aerosols.

Tuesday was October the eighth. We had a tight deadline if Santa's Train was to be ready on time. Every day that week, I was making inspections as well as chasing up craftsmen and materials. I had a skilled team constructing and decorating the tunnel, making it appear as though it

93

snaked through a mountainside. Occasionally it would emerge, in order to view one of my scenes by the railway track. Inclines and gentle falls would add to the experience of actually travelling to the North Pole.

There was little oversight from above, provided I kept to budget. Dave tended to stay away on other projects, gleaning only sufficient information to give progress reports to Brenda and HJ.

★ ★ ★

When the weekend arrived, I definitely felt prepared for a break. As usual it was a rapid rush to the shops on Saturday morning before most of them closed.

Our local grocer's stayed open every day for those provisions we all forgot to buy at the big stores. The goods were more expensive, yet there was a special feel whenever we entered the spacious room with its shelves crammed full of everything from light bulbs to cloth nappies and tins of Tom

Piper's Camp Pie.

The Comninoses were very friendly. They'd arrived soon after the war. It must have been difficult for them learning a new alphabet and language on top of adjusting to this strange land.

On Saturday afternoon, Sharon and I called in there on the way back from the playground with its slippery dip and roundabout.

'Could I have a half pound of butter, please, Elexis.'

The teenager cut a chunk off the large block in the glass-fronted refrigerator and wrapped it again. As usual she had an uncanny knack for judging it exactly right.

I noted some new Christmas cards on the magazine rack, next to one of those comics that Nick had mentioned. On one, Santa was wearing a full-length striped swimming costume and was holding a surf board. The caption read *Happy Christmas From Down Under*. I was about to buy a few to send home when I realised the futility. After all, we'd be there in person.

While Elexis put my piece of butter into a wrapper, Mrs Comninos returned from taking a crate of empty soft drink bottles out the back.

I greeted her. 'May I ask how you manage Christmas here away from the old country?'

The short woman with the always-smiling features wiped her hands on her apron and took a deep breath. The heavy lifting was taking its toll on her. She swept back her salt and peppered hair from her wrinkled forehead.

'It was difficult, those first few years, Miss Pamela. Ayios Vassileios came to visit Elexis and her sisters as is our tradition. He is our name for Santa. It took us some time to understand — is not the place where we celebrate the birth of our Lord. Is the people with who we share it. Family is most important. No?'

I took her calloused hand in mine
'This is so true, Mrs Comninos.'

I paid her for our purchases. She had

three daughters who took turns to assist her in the shop. It was open from six a.m. to ten p.m. and was the cornerstone for the blocks of houses around. It was also where people of all migrant nationalities came to gossip and for the latest scandal, mixing freely with local Aussies. Shops like this helped make our community live as one.

'Are you and your Sharon going out with the green man again tomorrow?' She winked, while Elexis hid her laugh behind an open hand.

'Green man? You mean Nick. Yes, as a matter of fact we are. He's taking us to a surprise place.'

'It's going to be an awfully awfully big adventure,' Sharon announced proudly.

I bent down to give her a kiss. So I was a part of the community now . . . at least as far as having a man calling on us went.

'Is good to see you with a special man, Pamela. We ladies . . . We should not be alone.'

97

At that moment Mr Comninos came in from the house at the back of the shop. He gave his wife a peck on the cheek, nodded to me then took a Wagon Wheel biscuit before disappearing again.

'Yes. We need our men and they need their chocolate,' she laughed as the door closed.

As we left, I wondered about that. She was part of the older generation. I didn't want another marriage. Sharon and I would be fine together without any males to complicate our lives.

⋆   ⋆   ⋆

Sunday saw 'the Green Man' arrive for our second outing. Nick told me that Gwen, the lady he'd help resuscitate the week before, had contacted him to pass on her thanks. She would be in hospital for another week but the prognosis was good. She was expected to make a full recovery, provided she took her new prescribed medication.

Sharon wrote her a special get well card. Nick promised to send it along with his own letter.

I'd brushed Sharon's hair until it shone in the spring daylight. My own hair was styled more casually and my panda-eye make-up was more subdued than I generally wore at work.

The rain during the night gave a fresh scent to everything in the street. It was going to be a day to remember.

Nick gave Sharon a large packet of sunflower seeds. She gave us a quizzical look.

'They're not for you, pumpkin. They're for our surprise friends. Do you have any guesses?'

'Are we going to a garden to plant them, Nick?'

'You'll have to wait, Sharon. But I can tell you that we're driving over the big bridge we saw last weekend.'

That had her excited. She clutched the seeds to her chest protectively as we started off. Our 'awfully big adventure' had begun.

We were headed for the north shore where the posh people lived — Sydney too had its north-south divide. That journey across the huge bridge was an event I'd remember for the rest of my life. I hoped Sharon would, too.

Nick appeared to be struggling with directions, explaining that he didn't come up this way very often. I offered to read the street directory book.

'A woman who can read maps? I'm impressed.'

I lifted it out of the glove box, deciding not to comment on the glimpsed photo before Nick closed the compartment door. It appeared to be of a woman with a young boy. He gave me the address where we were going. Quickly, I found it and was soon guiding him along the main streets threading through the suburbs into the semi-countryside.

When we arrived, Sharon was bursting with anticipation, repeatedly uttering that age-old catch-phrase of kiddies, 'Are we there yet?'

As we got out onto the footpath, I complimented Nick on his dress sense; a khaki and white shirt with dark brown pants.

'Mum helped me choose what to wear. Bearing in mind where we're going now, she suggested that lime green might cause some camouflage hassles. She keeps asking about the two of you. Wants to meet up for lunch.'

This did not bode well. 'She does realise we're friends, not . . . well, not anything more?'

'Of course. She's simply interested. You know what mums are like.'

Only too well, I thought.

Rounding a corner, Sharon saw our destination.

'That sign says *Park*. But what's that animal?'

'It's a koala, Sharon. Inside there are loads of animals and birdies. But only Aussie ones.'

'Birdies? That's what these seeds are for?'

'Shall we go in? My treat. And before

you protest, Pamela, you may buy us lunch. That way, we'll call it even. There's a café in there.'

I suspected I was getting the best part of the deal but accepted his suggestion.

Once past the turnstiles, I realised how vast this special Australian zoo was. Although some areas were fenced off, most weren't. An inquisitive four-foot-high kangaroo hopped over to say hello.

'Skippy!' exclaimed Sharon. I remembered the television show she had been watching. I'd brought my camera this time and spent the next hour taking photos of Sharon and the amazing beasts. She actually cuddled a koala bear — except I was told firmly by an attendant that they weren't really bears but marsupials with pouches.

There were flying foxes that were huge bats, wombats, Tasmanian devils, snakes (fortunately behind glass), black and yellow Corroboree frogs. We all marvelled at the budgies, parrots, cockatoos and multi-hued rosellas. Sharon was permitted to feed some of them the sunflower seeds.

Nick was snacking on some crisps after we'd had our lunch. Typical man. A huge head appeared over his shoulder between him and me. The crisps disappeared in an instant. We all jumped.

'You thieving so-and-so,' Nick yelled, thinking some man had stolen his snack. A huge bird with a long neck glared back. It was even taller than Nick. They faced off against one another, scant inches between nose and beak.

'It's an emu!' cried Sharon, clapping her hands. Nick didn't share her elation.

I managed a quick snap of the scene from *Crisp Fight at the OK Corral*.

'Damn thieving bird,' Nick muttered, conceding defeat. The emu crunched on the chips in its beak before turning and sauntering off, wiggling its bottom like Gina Lollobrigida on a movie set.

At that moment, a kookaburra commenced its raucous laugh causing Nick's expression to change from a frown to a grin.

'Looks like all the local birds have decided that it's Let's Pick on Nick Day,' I observed.

That gave us all a laugh.

Once home again, I closed the street directory to put it back in the glove box. It took only a second to see the photo that I'd noticed earlier was gone. He must have removed it, though I had no idea why. Nevertheless we'd had a fantastic day. I invited him in for a cuppa; he politely declined.

'Would you both fancy a trip to the Blue Mountains next Sunday?' he asked instead.

I was in two minds. This Sunday outing routine was becoming too regular. What's more, it was difficult to believe that any handsome young man would be so generous with his time, and money, yet not expect any more than a polite 'thanks'.

'Think we'll give it a break, Nick. I'm busy with work and I'd prefer to start planning our journey home; packing and such.'

'If that's what you want. How's about Thursday night? Carol singing?'

I reminded him we wouldn't be around at Christmas. 'What's the point?'

'Last time I heard, they sang carols in Manchester. 'Sides, we're performing at your shopping centre near the Waterfall Fountain, every Thursday evening from November fourteenth. You'll still be around then, won't you?' He grinned, pressing his point. 'Sharon would love the singing.'

He was right about that.

'We're not from your church, Nick,' I responded in a half-hearted attempt to dissuade him.

'No worries, Pamela. We welcome everyone, even pretty English ladies.'

It was obvious I was beaten. We made arrangements for him to collect us.

'Now, about Sunday?' He was nothing if not persistent.

'Don't push it, Mr Winters. I'll let you know. See you Thursday.'

Thinking about the carol singing, I was inspired to add something to the Santa Train ride. The first scene would be a northern European village scene with steep roofs and 'snow' all around. Why not have some mannequin singers dressed in woollen hats and scarves to serenade the train passengers? Some carols being sung in the background to set the ambience? Perfect.

You're a genius, Pamela, I told myself. Some of the vistas would have subtle night lighting, maybe with twinkling stars in the night sky, whereas others would be a cavalcade of bustling noise and brightly coloured lights.

The sensory experience of Santa's Train would be one that all the passengers would remember fondly for years to come. At least I hoped so.

★ ★ ★

It was a busy week preparing the Train. The track had to be laid along the winding path I'd mapped out. It was in a relatively small space, so the tight twists and turns meant that often only a foot or two of tunnel walls separated the track between different scenes. If this was what it was like to play with a Hornby 00 train set, I found myself envying boys.

My dedicated team shared my enthusiasm, asking advice regarding the best position for a rocking horse or a miniature fir tree. Inside the dark-painted tunnels we had installed lighting, both for working and for safety once the exhibit was up and running.

Brenda came to inspect progress. 'Walk me though the tunnel, Pamela,' she said.

We set off from the large annex from the main shopping mall. This was where the queues and ticket booth were located. Dave was in charge of this area and the signage. That suited me fine.

Entering the enclosed tunnel space, the lights suddenly went out. There was still illumination from the entrance yet I could sense panic starting to build.

'Sorry,' one of the electricians called out as light flooded the papier mâché-shrouded passageway again.

The tunnel was eight feet wide and high and there was a deliberately long stretch before the first scene. I wanted to give that sense of mystery and anticipation. It would take the train twenty seconds to reach the village. Paintwork and model construction was about half completed. My carol singers were dressed and in position.

'Looks almost real,' Brenda commented.

The next scene was the North Pole wasteland with its glaciers and whiteness everywhere. An artic owl hooted in a tree every few seconds.

'What are *they* doing there?' I asked Colin, one of my team. A family of penguins peered at us from an ice shelf.

'Dave's orders, Pamela.'

'Problems?' Brenda inquired.

'Penguins are only around the South Pole. Still, it's not meant to be scientifically accurate and it *is* Dave's idea for all of this.'

My tone was tinged with anger and cynicism. Nick was accurate to name me Sarcastic Lass.

Brenda examined my features in the half-light but said nothing. We moved on.

'This is the reindeer field where they eat and play,' I said. A sign pointing to Santa's Workshop was fixed amid the snow-covered grass.

We continued along. There was the workshop with singing elves, then Santa's living room with Mrs Claus rocking to and fro, a stack of letters in her hand. Finally there was the grotto where the train would allow the passengers to disembark to speak to Santa himself.

'I'm impressed, Pamela. Dave's vision is certainly going to be a winner.'

I ignored her statement, explaining that the photos taken of young visitors would be larger than the usual. 'The extra few cents will help defray the outlay. Furthermore, I've found a buyer for the electric train and track for after it's all dismantled.'

'What's the matter, Pamela? Whenever I mention Dave's name, you go funny.'

I couldn't contain my frustration any longer. Besides, Brenda was my friend. She'd understand.

'It's Dave. His idea for Santa's Train. There's something you need to . . . '

5

'There you two are.' It was Dave's voice. 'I've been searching for you everywhere.' He eyed me suspiciously before continuing in that brusque, take-charge manner of his. 'What do you reckon, Brenda? Bonza, if I do say so myself.'

'Yes, Dave. Very impressive. HJ will be pleased when I tell him how it's looking. I like the penguins. Now, Pamela. What were you about to say about Dave?'

I had to think quickly. 'Er . . . only that he's arranged to sell the train after we've finished using it.'

Brenda seemed a little perplexed. 'But I thought . . . '

'Got a good price for it too, didn't you, boss?'

'Er . . . yeah.' Dave didn't have a clue, but he was ready to take my lead.

'Course they tried to buy it cheap but I got them to agree to my price in the end.'

We talked for another ten minutes before Brenda said she had to leave for a meeting back at head office. She asked me to accompany her to her car.

Dave seemed edgy until Brenda explained it was about my new boyfriend and she simply wished to get the latest news from me.

'Boyfriend, eh Pamela? First I knew about him. Thought I was the only bloke in your life.'

As if, I thought. Not that Nick was my lover. Even so, he'd make a hundred of a lying jerk like Dave.

Brenda waited until we were out of earshot as we headed to the car park that was part of Waratah World. It was good to be away from my boss and the noise and dust of the construction site in the extension.

I gazed around at all the mothers gossiping or window shopping in the relative comfort of the undercover mini-city of shops and offices.

'Pamela. Is there anything that you wished to discuss about this project?'

I considered the tenuous position I was in. Ideally, I would need a decent reference from here for my next job in the UK.

'Only that I hope it will be a success; a swan song for my employment in Australia.'

'You're still leaving before Christmas? I'll be sad to say farewell. Nick will feel the same, I imagine.'

I needed to clarify our relationship. Why couldn't a man and a woman simply be friends?

'Nowt to do with Nick. He was aware of my plans from day one at your barbie . . . sorry, barbecue.'

'No hand-holding, kissing or sweet whispers in your ear?'

'Absolutely not. And none of that other stuff either. He's a sweet man, but love? Never!'

* * *

113

Tuesday evening saw an unexpected visitor; Nick. He'd brought us one of those newish cassette players with a tape labelled *Carols*.

'Thought you might enjoy hearing what our church choir are practising, even though you will probably recognise most of them. I reckoned it might help Sharon. Here are carbon copies of the lyrics as well.'

It was thoughtful of him and I said so.

'Would you care for a drink? A nice cup of tea, perhaps?'

He grinned. 'Funny how you English say that. You never call tea 'horrible' or 'insipid'.'

When I offered some biscuits, he called them 'bikkies'. Australians were a strange lot.

Sharon showed him Mrs de Luca's kittens, especially her favourite, Snowy. I'd tried to explain that she shouldn't think of Snowy as hers but that concept was difficult for her to understand.

I prayed that the loss of her kindy

friends and her familiar surroundings here would soon be forgotten, replaced by being with her loving grandparents and my sister's family.

★ ★ ★

When we sat down to listen to the tape late on Wednesday, I discovered Nick had chosen to include a pop song at the beginning. The strains of *Pamela, Pamela* echoed around the room.

'Mummy. He's singing about you,' exclaimed Sharon happily.

I hadn't had much time for pop music after I reached twenty, even though it had permeated life in the UK. I'd met a few famous artists in the clubs and casinos in Manchester following deregulation. Was this singer, Wayne Fontana, one of them? I wasn't certain.

After the carols began, it was clear Sharon was familiar with some of them. I guessed from kindy. I meant kinder-garten. In spite of my resolve I was being contaminated by Aussie-speak.

There was one song I didn't recall ever hearing though Sharon had; *The Carol Of The Birds*.

'It's 'Stralian, Mummy.'

Well, that explained it. The words and music were catchy and uplifting. However the bird names were mostly ones I had no idea about. Bellbirds? Brolgas? Perhaps Nick might help.

★   ★   ★

On Thursday, we were there with the other two dozen or so carollers. Obviously it was awkward for Sharon. She was almost five but being with so many strangers was daunting. She was more clingy than normal.

Nick was very attentive, introducing us to a number of the group including some youngsters. The number of new names had me lost very rapidly so I just relaxed into the task at hand.

I did agree to the Blue Mountain trip. After all, we only had a few more weeks to visit some of the parts around Sydney and, apart from some unanswered questions about Nick's behaviour, he had been a perfect gentleman to me and a brilliant companion to Sharon. By perfect, I meant he hadn't made one romantic suggestion to me.

It was in some ways an insult. I regarded myself as being attractive, even desirable, yet this attentive and good-looking guy was keeping his distance. Was I that unapproachable?

★   ★   ★

My little girl and I went to church on Saturday evening so we'd have all day free on Sunday. The trip to the Blue Mountains would be a long one. I'd done my best to prepare Sharon. Nick told me he had a plan to help too.

Driving west, we eventually saw them in the distance. They were a hazy blue.

'It's the eucalypt oils evaporating

from the gum trees, Pamela. Spectacular, isn't it?'

I had to agree. Australian native flowers and trees were such a different green.

'I can see the attraction, Nick. There's a beauty here — just a different type to home.'

'There was a poet called Dorothea Mackellar at the turn of the century. She was young, in the UK and very homesick.

'*I love a sunburnt country, a land of sweeping plains,*

'*Of ragged mountain ranges, of droughts and flooding rains.*

'Well that's how it begins, I think. I guess being homesick doesn't just apply to English women. You've spent only a short few years here but for Sharon, it's been almost half her life. I wonder where she'll come to regard as 'home.''

I hadn't considered that. Was I doing the right thing, taking her away from the place she knew? Even her memories of my family were based on photos.

Nick continued his reminiscences.

'Our family used to come up here a lot. My dad's into amateur radio, talking to blokes all over the country . . . other places too, like Japan and the States. He built our first telly in fifty-seven when television began over here. For years, we were the only people with television on our street.

'Anyway, we had a radio set up in our car. We'd drive up somewhere high like Mount Tomah and picnic. My sister and I would explore the bush while Mum read and Dad contacted people, often doing contests to see how many other radio 'hams' he could speak to.'

Nick hadn't discussed his family much before. It was good to find out a little more about him. Also, I began to notice a change in my attitude to the countryside. It was unfair to compare it to England with its lush greenery. Each had their own special qualities. Nick had opened my eyes.

I turned to examine him more closely. He was concentrating on the road but his peripheral vision must have given me away as he glanced over.

'What's the attraction, Pamela?'

'You,' I replied quite deliberately. 'You're a decent man, Mr Nick Winters. Kind, helpful and . . . and you deserve to find a woman who loves you and appreciates all the things that you have to offer.' I realised it was getting a tad too serious so I added, 'And one who can teach you to dress properly. I can see the elastic garters in those long socks you're wearing.'

'So you were looking at my legs. I thought so. That means there's no problem if I look at yours.'

Would I object if he did? Probably not. I liked what I saw in him and hoped he'd be proud to be seen in my company also.

I turned back to the road and adjusted the side vent windows so that the breeze blowing through, tousled my hair.

Nick was wearing a white nylon shirt, grey shorts and white socks. His legs and arms were tanned, the dark hair on his lower arms arranged almost as if he combed it.

Unlike the fringe I preferred to cover my forehead, Nick combed his back. There was a slight wave to it. He removed his sunglasses as a large cloud shaded the sun. Those green eyes were almost unearthly.

A car passed us with a woman, man and two boys. I guessed it was a family. Would they think the same of us, just like that poor lady who'd had the heart problem? That reminded me.

'How is Gwen? The lady on the ferry.'

'Recovering well. I spoke to her daughter the other day. Seems that Gwen is a producer of television shows. She's taking more of a back seat now. Her son is taking over.' He checked the rear view mirror. 'Appears that a certain beautiful girl might be getting bored, Pamela. If you look in the glove-box, there's a game for you and Sharon to play. You each have a card and you call out 'Spotto' if you see any of the items. My sis and I played it all the time.'

★　★　★

By the time we reached Glenbrook in the mountain foothills, Sharon was well ahead. She only had one more item to cross off her card.

We pulled into a camping ground for an early lunch. 'Spotto caravan!' she called out, proudly marking the picture on the card. 'I've won.'

'That's fab.' Nick leaned over to see my card. 'Poor old Mummy has another three to find.'

'Not so much of the 'old', Mr Winters,' I chided him, before a playful punch on the arm. It was the first time we'd touched since I'd put my hand on his, stopping him from leaving that first night. In spite of my earlier misgivings, it felt right. *Friends touch one another, don't they*, I thought, justifying my actions.

During lunch, Nick indicated the

different plants around us. The waratahs and kangaroo paws were colourful and there were various species of gum trees. Sharon kept an eye out for koalas but didn't see any. Then she remembered about the carol with the bird names in it.

'Are there any around here?' she asked him.

He listened for a moment. 'Bellbirds. Can you hear them?'

I listened. Among the squawks of parrots and the chirping of flocks of budgies, there was a beautiful ringing sound. It had been there all the time, though I hadn't noticed.

'Wow,' I said.

'They're mentioned in the second verse.

'*Down where the tree ferns grow by the river*

'*There where the waters sparkle and quiver,*

'*Deep in the gullies bell-birds are chiming*

'*Softly and sweetly their lyric notes*

rhyming,' he sang then Sharon joined in for the chorus,

'*Orana! Orana! Orana to Christmas Day.*'

'What do bellbirds look like?' she demanded.

'Not sure,' Nick replied. 'They're secretive. Keep to themselves, unlike bloody emus. Sorry, shouldn't have said that in front of you, Sharon.'

'It's OK, Nick. Mummy uses naughty words.'

I blushed. Miss Big Ears had struck again.

Following our lunch — complete with inch-long orange and black bull ants — we set off on the winding road to Katoomba. Before long I began to feel cooler and closed my side vent window.

'Told you to bring a cardie,' our driver told me.

'We did, smarty pants.' I poked my tongue out playfully. Sharon reached into a bag for them. 'And they're called cardigans, Mr Winters.'

Sharon followed the banter quietly, smiling.

After stopping Nick struggled into his own colourful jumper with a roll neck. It mussed up his hair, but that wasn't all. The jumper had a smiling possum's face on the chest. Even Sharon giggled.

'My mum enjoys knitting,' he explained, a resigned look on his face.

Eventually we pulled up in Katoomba, at a spot overlooking a gorgeous vista of trees in a valley far below.

Nick pointed out a rock formation over the guard rail. 'The Three Sisters.'

'It's very high,' Sharon observed apprehensively, staying well away from the edge.

'Have to agree,' I added. Maybe I should have mentioned my fear of heights. The Lake District back home never seemed as daunting.

Australia was young in one way, being only sixty-eight years old as a union of separate states yet the panorama before me suggested it had been here forever. I could easily believe that there were paths down there that no man, white or aboriginal, had ever walked upon. Australia was raw, primitive and untamed.

★　★　★

Nick took us to a swimming pool at a place called Lawson on the way back to Sydney.

'My family would come here every November for a radio ham convention day. Dad was in his element with all his electronics mates. Carol and I amused ourselves exploring. There's a waterfall down that way, but it's a long walk. Perhaps another time?' He noticed my passive expression. 'Or perhaps not.'

There was a pause before he began striding off. 'Come on, you two. It's too cold for the pool but there is a fairy glen I want to show you.'

'Fairies! Will we see any?' Sharon asked.

'I doubt it, pumpkin. They only come out at night. I thought you'd know that.'

'Sorry, Nick. I forgetted — er, forgot.'

'But there is a tiny waterfall and their special pool where they swim. Shall we go see it?'

We passed by the Olympic-sized pool. There were a number of brave souls in there, swimming or sunbathing. Better them than me. I figured Dave's penguins would feel right at home.

Going swimming in the great outdoors. That was one of the promises made by the Australian Consulate guy when he'd interviewed Frank and me. Strangely, he'd never mentioned Sydney's oppressive humidity in the hot summer, flies that wanted to eat you alive and disgusting cockroaches. I wondered if we might get compensation for misleading advertising.

Yes, of course, Mrs Grant. Here are those two years of your life back. Please accept our most sincere apologies for any inconvenience.

We left the pool area behind to trek up a gentle grassed incline with a rivulet gurgling alongside our gravel path. All around there was birdsong and the changing scents of flowers. The waters were as clear as could be.

'Look. There's a dragonfly.' Nick pointed. He appeared eager to share this place of childhood adventures. He sounded more like a boy than a grown man with responsibilities; almost like an Aussie Peter Pan.

The dragonfly fluttered over the stream, darting from one side to the other, its iridescent wings sparking like miniature rainbows in the afternoon sun. The water course itself was about a yard wide. Up ahead it split, flowing from the waterfall to encircle the treasure Nick and Carol had discovered years ago.

'Not many people realise it's here. Some locals look after it, keep the grass under control. We used to jump over to it.'

'Can we please jump, too? I'm a good jumper,' Sharon said, pretending to be Skippy.

'Of course. Here's a narrow bit.' Nick helped her across to the concrete relief replica of Australia. It was about three yards wide in both directions. There was a Tasmania also, separated by swiftly flowing water from the mainland. Painted labels in metal were fixed in different locations with tiny landmarks on them.

I explained what it was to Sharon, showing her where we lived. We moved around the mini-continent.

'Watch me. I'm on Can . . . ber . . . ra.'

'And I'm on Ayers Rock. What about you, Pamela?'

I giggled. 'Brisbane. Funny. I've never been to Brisbane before.'

'What's it like over there, Mummy?'

'It's on the coast, very close to the — Oh no. Too slippery. Help!'

The water was only a few inches deep, yet the splash and landing on my bottom ensured I was soaked, even my hair.

'It's . . . it's fr . . . fr . . . freezing.' I tried to stand on the round pebbles of the stream bed.

'Fresh mountain water,' said Nick, laughing heartily. 'It snowed up here two weeks ago. Come on, soggy lady. Allow me to help you out.'

Nick took my the hands and pulled me from the running waters. I slipped again. He caught me, then I fell forward into his arms, against his body.

For a moment, it felt great to be encircled by the arms of a man once again before I remembered whose arms they were. I pulled away demurely. The scent of his aftershave lingered.

'Sorry, Nick. That shouldn't have happened.'

'Darn right, it shouldn't. Now I'm soaking too.'

'We'll dry off quickly enough,' I suggested, conscious that my underwear might take longer.

'There's a towel in my car,' Nick

offered. 'Used to be a Scout. Always prepared. You never know when you might have a pretty mermaid around.'

The walk back was subdued. Had I crossed a line? It was bad enough to leave a few toys and handbags here when we returned home; however I was very aware about leaving a man who'd become more than a friend to me and Sharon.

It was October the twentieth; just over two months until Christmas. Already I was beginning to doubt my resolve not to become involved. In another place, another time, I could envisage us as a proper family. I could actually overlook the fact that he was a colonial who talked funny.

Nick was great with Sharon. She liked him . . . a lot. Moreover, he made me feel fine about myself with his genuine compliments about my appearance, clothes and my personality.

He took an interest in my work too. My ex never had. In some ways, Nick was an Aussie James Bond — although not as sophisticated. At times his immaturity came through, yet was that a bad thing? I was the other way, often too blinking serious for my own good. Even I needed a laugh now and then. It was a pity his jokes and puns were so dreadful.

★   ★   ★

By the time we headed back down to Penrith at the base of the mountain range, both Sharon and I were sleepy. It had been a wonderful, if wet day.

I was closing my eyes, confident in Nick's driving, when there was a frantic cry of 'Mummy!' from behind my seat.

Immediately I was awake. Scant inches from my face, a huge spider dropped down from the sun visor onto my lap. It was at least four inches across.

Sharon's scream was nothing compared to mine. Held by the seat belt, all I could do was scrunch up and vainly try to brush it away.

'Nick. S . . . S . . . save me.'

6

Too late, I realised that we were on a winding road with a steep drop on the left hand side.

To Nick's credit, the shrieks only partially distracted him from his concentration on driving. He slowed and pulled safely into a lay-by.

'What's the problem, Pamela?'

'Sp . . . sp . . . spider,' I gasped, my body tensed to breaking point.

'Where?'

'Are you blind? On my dress. Get it off. Now!'

Nick laughed. I couldn't believe his attitude. I could have strangled him at that moment if I weren't so petrified.

Calmly he reached across to the offending monster then, without any alarm, coaxed the creature to run up his bare, hairy arm.

I shuddered. What if it attacked him?

Australian spiders could kill. Even I knew that.

'Watch out! It'll bite you.'

I sensed that Sharon was sharing my apprehension and concern for Nick's safety.

'Relax, you two. It's not a funnel-web or a red back. They're much smaller. This is a harvestman. It's big and scary-looking but it's not aggressive. See.' He put a finger near the ghastly arachnid. It didn't move.

'But it's gigantic.' I was calming down, entranced. It was as wide as my hand.

'Must have crawled in at Glenbrook. I'll let him go now.' Nick opened the car door and dropped the creature gently onto the dirt. It scuttled off.

'We have a load of nasties in Australia. It's important to understand which ones are dangerous, otherwise you'll spend your life permanently petrified.'

'Then it's a good thing we're not staying. The most dangerous animal in England is a cheesed-off hedgehog.'

* * *

It was dark by the time we arrived home. We'd had some food at a cafe on the way. Nick had insisted on paying.

'Thursday night again for carol practice, you two?' he asked, pulling up next to the side gate.

I swivelled my neck around to Sharon. The mercury street light wasn't great but I could see her nod enthusiastically.

'Yes. We'd love to come. And we've had a lovely day, although I suspect that a certain young girl is quite tired.' *Also someone else needs to get her still-damp clothes off*, I thought, grateful that the bench seat was vinyl.

'Wonder if I could ask you a favour, Pamela? Unlike me, you've been to France. In fact, none of our language staff have left Oz. How would you feel about coming to one or two of my classes and talk about your impressions of the country and its people? Maybe describe Paris to the kids?'

I considered his request. He'd been so fantastic, showing us around.

'Just realised. Dumb of me. You're at work on school days.'

'No, that's OK. I can take time off. I have holidays built up.' I mentally checked my schedule for the week ahead. 'Wednesday would be good. I have coloured slides I took in Paris, at Christmas 1963, the year before I became pregnant. Can you sort out a slide projector?'

'That sounds fab. Projector's no problem. It'll be a treat for my students, and me too.'

★   ★   ★

Next day, at work, I told Dave I'd be having Wednesday off. He was not a happy bunny. Nevertheless, it wasn't up to him. Brenda had given me the OK and her word was final.

The first Christmas vista was giving me problems. I needed an impact; some aspect that made the children and

136

parents say 'Wow. This is really special. We're going to the North Pole.' Plastic penguins alone were not going to cut it.

'What's so important that you're taking a day off my project, Pamela?' Dave asked.

I wondered why he was uptight about it. I'd been supervising the placement of the elves in Santa's workshop. My aim was to make it bustling and happy, though not too loud. Some laughter would lighten the soundtrack looped on a tape recorder.

'I'm headed to a school to do some teaching, if you must know.'

'Ha! What could you teach, Pamela? Bloody make-up? You might be a half-decent looking sheila but you've hardly got any brains under that pop-star haircut of yours.'

I kept my calm, literally thinking of England. I was used to his insults and demeaning comments although lately they'd got worse. It was as though he wasn't making any pretence at common decency with me any longer. What would my alter-ego Sarcastic Lass do when confronting such an evil super-villain?

I patted and smoothed my hair, drawing strands of my page boy cut through my fingers and across my cheeks. 'At least I still have my hair, Dave. What's your excuse?'

That elicited quite a vocal response from my boss. Even if he tried to hide his bald spot with a comb-over, Dave was looking more and more like Robin Hood's Friar Tuck every time he appeared.

'You . . . you'll get yours, lady. One day I'll make you pay for that.' His voice was vindictive and spiteful. It was also loud enough to attract the attention of three workmen putting up some electrical ducting.

Despite Dave's bluster, we both understood who had won this little exercise in humiliation. There was no possibility that I'd let him take any more from me. Santa's Train was all he'd ever get. Unfortunately I sensed he had other plans, and would use them when I least expected it.

I heard that afternoon about Wednesday's briefing with HJ. Obviously he wanted me there to do his presentation for him under the pretext that he'd done all the work.

Dave didn't have a clue about 'his' brilliant idea. If he made a hash of it on Wednesday explaining things he had no clue about, I, for one, wouldn't be losing any sleep.

Finding out about the teacher side of Nick would be interesting. I'd speculated about it with Sharon as I examined the slides of my younger life.

There was a tiny viewer with batteries providing the light, so it was a tedious but nostalgic task in choosing which slides I'd show. After each one, Sharon would use the viewer, followed by more insatiable questions.

Nick picked me up from Sharon's kindergarten in his car. A student had written *Wash Me* in large letters on the rear window — in reverse so that it read properly when Nick viewed it in his mirror.

Listening to him in class impressed me. The pupils were attentive and respectful to both him and me. When I'd left school almost fifteen years before, the teachers were much more into strict discipline than he seemed to be.

Nick's school taught French, Latin and German languages with one teacher doing Japanese. Apparently he was the only one in the state. Studying European languages was interesting if hardly practical. France and Germany were halfway around the world, whereas ancient Rome . . .

Nick made introductions in French to each of his classes. His accent was different to Parisian French so I struggled a little.

I showed them my slides, using simple French phrases whenever I could. 'Who recognises this? Qu'est-ce c'est?' I asked the boys and girls.

'La Tour Eiffel,' one girl responded.

'Why is it white all around?' another said.

'Snow. La neige. It was a very cold winter. Down to ten degrees Fahrenheit.'

I imagined it never went below thirty in Sydney.

'I'd love to see snow. What does it feel like? Does it smell?' Questions came thick and fast.

I digressed to talk about my experiences with snow, especially the magical absence of sound when it was falling. They were fascinated.

I enquired, 'Who's actually seen snow?'

No one put up their hand apart from one girl.

'I used to live in Katoomba, Miss. I saw it once but it melted before it hit the ground. It'd be super to see it again.'

That's when I had my brainwave. Christmas and snow were synonymous to many Aussies; Christmas cards, fluffy stuff called Santa-snow you sprayed on the decorated tree in the lounge room or on windows, movies with Bing Crosby.

I'd give the visitors to Santa's Train a taste of the Arctic as they passed the snow-clad village. Not artificial flakes, the real thing; freezing cold flakes falling all around. There were logistics to arrange, but it would work. And I had the perfect guy in mind to grant my snow-white wish.

That evening, I put pen to Basildon Bond, writing to my parents and my sister. It would cost more to post them airmail, but there was no point sending them by ship as we'd be back in the UK well before the letters would arrive.

★ ★ ★

During Thursday's carol rehearsal, Sharon and I were much more confident with the seasonal songs, even the Aussie one. There was a wondrous uplifting ambience as we all joined in, especially with the harmonies. Nick had brought a picture book of Australian birds. He pointed out the carrawong, lorikeets and bellbirds as well as the cute dancing brolga mentioned in the carol.

Some of the others in the chorus admitted they'd not seen photos of some of them before.

'You've been invited for lunch on Sunday at Mum and Dad's. The weather forecast wasn't ideal for going out so when I mentioned I'd be seeing you both, they made the suggestion. What do you reckon? We could go ten-pin bowling after if you wish.'

It was an awkward moment.

'Your parents know there's nothing romantic between us, don't they? A lunch invite ... it seems a little strange.'

I gave it a moment before agreeing. I was a big girl now and I was as intrigued to meet them as they apparently were to meet me. In addition, the idea of having a meal prepared by someone else was very appealing. I wasn't the best cook in the world. My own mother had often declared I could burn water. Lunch with Nick's family? What could possibly go wrong?

★   ★   ★

On Saturday morning, Sharon and I went to our local High Street. We'd not been for a while and it felt sad in a way that we'd be leaving soon, saying goodbye to our friends and the church congregation. Although divorce was frowned upon technically, the reverend had supported us in every way he could.

The milkman had left our pint outside the door as usual yet I decided we'd need another bottle to help make the dessert Sharon loved. Condensed milk wasn't the same. Also I wanted to make enquiries for our flights back home.

We visited the same travel agent we'd been to before, a bright, freckle-faced

144

teenager called Darleen. All was fine until she told us the cost.

'How much?' I said in surprise. The ticket prices had seemingly increased a lot since I'd enquired two months before.

'There's been a recent price increase, Pamela. Plus it is December. School holidays as well as lots of people wanting to fly over there for Christmas. Supply and demand, I believe it's called.'

'Da — ' I began before remembering little Miss Big Ears was seated next to me. 'Drat and bother,' I said instead. It didn't feel as satisfying. Swear words definitely had their place in the world, if only to relieve frustration.

'What about Qantas?'

She checked her sheaves of papers then made a phone call. 'It's almost the same. Twenty dollars cheaper for the two of you.'

BOAC and Qantas were the only two airlines flying direct via Asia. Pan-Am went via America, however it took longer and was more expensive.

I remembered the flight that brought us here. Sharon was only two and despite Frank being with us, I was the one chasing her up and down the aisle. Another passenger commented as we disembarked that I'd walked to Australia.

I only had seven hundred dollars set aside for the flights but I could manage the difference with judicious budgeting. At least, that was my plan.

'Shall I reserve your seats? The deposit is refundable, however I'll need the final amount three weeks before the flight.'

I agreed, hoping I was doing the right thing for both of us. It would be one of those life-changing decisions, for Sharon especially. I'd already screwed things up marrying Frank and was conscious of further complicating our lives. Sometimes being a sole parent with all the responsibilities and decisions falling on my shoulders alone, made life very difficult.

'Smoking or non-smoking?'

'Non please, Darleen.' And just like that I'd sealed our fate. It made me a little nauseous to accept that. We were going home; the great Australian adventure had been a failure.

Leaving the agency, I was still upset and distracted. So much so that I didn't respond when Sharon first tugged my skirt. When she did it a second time, I stared down at her.

'What is it, kitten?'

'Over there, Mummy. It's Nick.'

I scanned the throng of shoppers bustling along the footpath. A double-decker bus blocked the view for a moment, then two delivery vans. And there he was. He was wearing those green shorts. How could I have missed him?

There was another person he was talking to by all appearances; a young woman with striking platinum blonde hair. What was more surprising was the boy walking with them.

My mind jumped to a conclusion — one that wasn't logical but made sense. *So that's why you couldn't see us on Saturdays, Mr Nick Winters.* There was another woman to keep him busy. Judging by the way he was holding her hand, they were very chummy indeed. The woman may have bleached her hair but, I decided, she was the one on the photo in the glove box. The red-haired boy was certainly the same.

'Shall we say hello?' Sharon said innocently.

'No, sweetheart. They look too busy. We'll see Nick tomorrow.'

Once again I was in two minds about my teacher friend. He had never told me he wanted more from me; in fact, Nick was the ultimate gentleman. Why then, was I feeling jealous of this mystery companion of his? Was she his ex and the boy his son? Was that the reason that there had been a child seat belt fitted?

Nick Winters was an enigma. I was wondering what the hell was going on . . . and how were the two of us involved?

7

It was the last Sunday in October. The rain was set to stay with us all day. Nick wasn't due until midday so Sharon and I were playing Kerplunk as we waited. It had come out last year and I'd bought it her for the previous Christmas.

We were already dressed from church and, in spite of getting our legs wet, our raincoats and brollies had done the trick. My hair was frizzy due to the humidity, although I'd made an effort for Nick's sake.

Nick was on time as usual. Reliability wasn't a problem. Keeping secrets was another matter.

'You looking forward to ten-pin bowling, Sharon?' he said as we buckled up. Sharon had become quite adept at it though Nick always checked.

'I . . . I don't know what it is,' Sharon admitted.

'I've been thinking about that idea, Nick. The bowling balls will be too heavy. She's not strong.'

'I'm not that much of a thicko, Pamela. There's a kiddy-sized set of lanes alongside the adult ones. I've booked us in for four o'clock.' He twisted his head to speak to Sharon. 'It's like skittles, pumpkin. Ever play that?'

Sharon looked blank. 'I . . . I don't think so.'

Nick began to explain, getting her even more confused with his school-teacher explanation. Seeing her distress, I calmed things down.

'It's sort of like a really big Kerplunk.' That satisfied her apprehension. Her frown turned into a smile.

Nick shrugged his shoulders, admitting he'd got it wrong. 'Sorry. It's hard to talk to young children. I never see any — apart from your Sharon, of course.'

And that boy from yesterday, I thought.

I'd made Sharon promise not to say anything about spying on Nick and the platinum blonde. She was generally fine with keeping quiet about some things though she was just a child. If she did inadvertently spill the beans, I wondered how Nick would react; denial, or playing down the relationship?

We drove in silence for a few blocks before Nick spoke.

'You're not so chatty today, Pamela, Pamela.'

'Bit of a headache. And please don't call me that. It's very irritating.' I wasn't in the greatest of moods.

'Apologies . . . I didn't mean to upset you. Perhaps you could tell me what you two did with yourselves yesterday?'

'Yesterday? We walked down to Summer Hill shops. Actually booked our flights home.'

'Yes,' called out Sharon from the back seat. 'We're going on an aeroplane like on the jelly packet. Whoosh. Right up into the sky.'

'Oh. Then you're still leaving?'

151

'Of course we are. Sixteenth of December. What about your Saturday, Nick? What did you do? Marking books? Mowing the lawn? Shopping?'

He glanced at me staring at him, nonchalantly.

'Er. Nothing much. Stayed in all day.' He rubbed his nose, abstractly.

Another uncomfortable pause in our normally lively conversation, interrupted only by the squeaky sound of the windshield wipers.

'Who'll be there at your parents' place?'

'Only Mum and Dad.'

'Not your sister?'

Nick replied in a terse voice. 'Carol? She's no longer around. It's best not to mention her name. There's been . . . Well. Don't bring her up. Even hearing her name is painful for them. OK?'

I wondered if she'd passed away; some illness or accident. I'd follow Nick's advice. There was no point upsetting his parents.

'Whatever you say, Nick.' I sighed.

This was shaping up to be one of those days when I wished we'd stayed at home. I wondered again about the reason we were going there.

★ ★ ★

The Winters' home was a detached weatherboard house with a small front garden behind a brick wall. There was an oleander tree growing by the steps to the front door. I remembered they were poisonous.

Nick dashed out to open the gates on the drive, allowing Sharon and me to appraise it. It appeared to be freshly painted in pink, with royal blue trim on the gutters and window frames and a blue tiled roof. It was on a quiet street with a bus stop and grocer's shop opposite.

When Nick returned, his hair dripping wet, I had to comment. 'I can see that you've inherited your parents' colour sense.'

Whether he regarded that as a

compliment, I wasn't certain. He parked behind a big new Valiant car on the concrete driveway at the side of the house. The Valiant was under a car port.

'I'll lead. You two follow. The rain's easing off, I think. Watch you don't slip, Pamela. Mum prefers visitors at the front door.'

We left our raincoats in the car and ran, crowding together under the metal canopy over the doorway at the top of the steps. The house name was *Belvoir*, a French name meaning beautiful view. It was also the name of a castle near Nottingham; some ancestral connection, I surmised. Nick had told me that his mother's family came from there.

As Nick fumbled for his keys, the door opened. Mrs Winters appeared to be in her late forties. It was hard to tell, as people seemed older than they actually were in this harsh climate. Her hair was dyed chocolate brown and she held herself upright as she greeted us. Her apron lay bundled on a chair in the bedroom to our left. The crimson lipstick and rouge were striking, though her welcoming smile put my mind at ease.

First impressions were encouraging. In France there'd be two kisses on each cheek, or even more. In Australia it was a polite handshake for me and Sharon. She and I appraised one another.

Mr Winters stood behind his wife, awkwardly balancing on one foot then the other. Nick had mentioned that he had gout from time to time. His shirt wasn't completely tucked in.

'My mum and dad,' said Nick by way of introductions.

Mrs Winters tisked. 'Nancy and Arthur. Pleased to meet you.' She then glared at Nick. 'They can hardly call us Mum and Dad, can they? Sometimes you're as thoughtless as your father.'

Nick blushed.

I tried to play it down and give Nick some support. 'Men, eh? They're the same the world over. They do have their uses, though.'

'Of course, Pamela. I'm very proud of my boys, especially Nick being a teacher. A pity he made some bad choices with his wife. I never liked her, you know. Too snooty by half.'

In my limited experience, there was always a moment between a mother and a new woman in her son's life. 'Is he good enough for my little bunnykins?' — even when bunnykins was twenty-six years old like my Nick. *Will she hurt him or spend all his money?* That sort of thing. It was similar to establishing a pecking order in a hen-house of chooks (as Aussies called them).

'Your son has been extremely kind to us, Nancy. He's been showing us around Sydney before we return to England in just over a month.'

Nancy appeared shocked.

'You're leaving him already?'

'We are simply friends, Nancy. I thought he would have explained that.'

Nick's mum relaxed visibly.

'Of course you are. You're obviously

much older than him. Mid- thirties?'

I kept my smiling face rigid. 'Twenty-nine.'

The ice was broken. 'Shall we all have a nice cup of tea before lunch? And a chat?'

'Yes, that sounds good,' I agreed.

Nancy took my hand to lead me through to the lounge room. All was right with the world . . . at least for the moment. Later, when Nick and I were alone, things wouldn't be as pleasant. I was already deciding which expletives I'd use.

★   ★   ★

Lunch was quite an affair. Sunday lunches often were here. There were cold slices of lamb with hot vegetables and mint sauce. It transpired that Arthur grew the potatoes himself in their back garden. There was an orange vegetable I'd seen in the greengrocers, though I'd never bought it. As far as I knew, pumpkin was fed to pigs back home, yet it was a delicacy over here.

Nancy declared proudly that her pumpkin scones were famous among her friends. Pumpkin scones? I shuddered. I hoped they weren't on offer for afternoon tea. There was also some insipid pale green pear- shaped thing called a choko. It grew on vines, I was told.

The pumpkin was lovely. The choko was not. It was green mush and although I pushed mine around the plate, Sharon politely ate it all.

'Rhubarb and custard for dessert,' our hostess announced after we cleared away the leftovers and dirty plates. The kitchen sink was on the other side of the house, near the bathroom. It seemed that when the house was built in the early 1900s, the idea of water in the kitchen was a step too far.

Afterwards, we all adjourned to the lounge room; two modern settees with cloth over foam cushions, plus a recliner. The television in the corner was the one built by Arthur eleven years earlier. It remained switched off, as did the large Bakelite radio. Outside the rain had returned with a vengeance, splattering against the curtained windows as though it wished to join us inside.

On the mantelpiece over a boarded-up fire grate, there were eight *Happy Anniversary* cards.

Sharon snuggled up to me on one settee with Nick and his mother on the other, at right angles to us. Arthur had moved his recliner around so that it was in front of the television screen.

Nancy started the interrogation. Actually, that was unfair. I was a guest here. They simply wanted to hear about the latest woman in Nick's life.

'Tell us a little about yourself, Pamela. You're from England?'

I relaxed back onto the seat. At the same time, a Siamese jumped up to my lap, making me tense again. He quickly found a home with Sharon, though. She had a way with cats.

'Manchester. It's in the north-west.

Near Liverpool.'

'Manchester United,' Arthur interrupted. 'Not that I follow soccer. More a Magpies fan, myself.' It was the local rugby league team. I didn't know any more than that.

'I remember we used to send food parcels, after the war. Of course you had it bad over there. Arthur here was in the army, but we never had all that bombing you had. The worst thing that happened here was the bombing of Darwin and finding a Jap submarine in Sydney harbour.'

'My parents sent me to live with my grandmother in the country. A place called Bromyard. I don't remember much about those years.'

Suddenly I had a vision of darkness and moving things touching me all over. There was this horrible smell, too.

'Are you all right, Pamela?' It was Nick. 'You just whimpered.'

'Did I? I didn't realise. My apologies.'

'And you've gone all pale, dearie.

Perhaps a glass of water?' Nancy was leaning forward. Her hand was on my knee.

I felt terrible. 'Yes, please.'

Nick went to fetch one. Everyone was staring at me. I was more concerned with Sharon and her reaction.

Arthur noticed, and asked her if she liked cats. I was grateful for his intervention.

'Yes, Mr Winters. I love them. Why has she got chocolate on her face and paws?'

'He's a special kind of cat called a Siamese. Christmas has a funny miaow, too. Listen.' He leaned forward. 'Speak, Christmas.'

The cat miaowed. Obviously it was a party trick.

'Mummy! He sounds like a baby. How awfully strange. And how can you tell he's a boy cat?'

Oh no. Boys and girls again.

'I'll explain later, Sharon,' I told her for the dozenth time, sensing her frustration at my reluctance to answer a simple question. Her curiosity was going to be a problem — but not as much as this 'awfully' habit of hers.

Although I still felt queasy, I persevered in distracting Sharon. 'Christmas. That's an unusual name, Arthur. Why choose that?'

'It was Nicky's fault. When he was younger, he wanted Christmas all year round so his mother, bless her, suggested we call his new kitten Christmas. Never mind that I still hear the bloke next door laughing when I'm outside, calling out 'Come on, Christmas'.'

'It could be worse,' I replied with a grin. 'My sister's cat is called Fluffy-Wuffy.'

That brought smiles to everyone's faces.

'I must say you're a much nicer woman than Nick's wife was. She was quite arrogant, you know. American, though I'm certain they're not all as bad as her. Nick prefers women with accents. Always has.'

Well, that was a revelation. Was that what attracted him to me? It sounded so shallow.

Nancy continued to talk. 'You were married too, I believe? Not one of those unmarried mothers that seem to be everywhere these days. It's such a shame, especially for the kiddies.'

That sounded quite judgemental, although unhappily it was true. That's why I kept my wedding ring on, to signal that my daughter was legitimate. I felt I was a coward for doing so. Why should any mother be judged in such a way?

Nick returned with a glass of iced water. I took a few sips.

'Maybe you're getting the flu?' he suggested.

Last I heard, whimpering wasn't one of the symptoms. No, it was something else . . . something I wanted to forget.

We continued to talk about my life here and what I noticed different about the two countries. There was genuine interest there. I chose to switch the

163

conversation back to them.

'Outside you have the Belvoir name for your lovely house. Nick said your family used to live near there.' I was feeling much better now.

Nancy sat up. 'That's right. Have you been near there in your travels?'

'No, I'm afraid not. Maybe we will when we get back. Despite what you might think, England's a big place to explore. Lots of cities and towns.'

Just then, Christmas reached out a paw, catching his claws on my pantyhose just above the knee. It was embarrassing as they began to ladder. I adjusted my skirt as best, I could.

Nancy kindly pretended not to notice.

'Nick mentioned you're working at Waratah World where they're doing the extension. We were over there only last week, weren't we, Arthur? Are you a salesgirl . . . sorry, woman?'

'No. I'm actually designing the Christmas attraction, Santa's Train. Perhaps you've heard of it?' I didn't feel it was boasting, simply a statement of fact.

It did apparently alter Nancy's opinion of me, though. Arthur's too. They both expressed delight and praise.

'We've seen the advertisements over there. It sounds like a wonderful attraction. I'd love to take my little one there.'

I noticed a look of annoyance cross Arthur's face. He touched his wife on her arm.

'Nancy. You know what we agreed.' His voice was calm yet firm.

'Yes . . . yes. I understand but . . . it will be Christmas and . . . '

'No buts, Nancy. We made a decision and nothing's changed.' Saying that, he sat back in the recliner and took out his pipe.

It was obviously a touchy subject; one that I shouldn't find out about. Not that I wanted to. Life was complicated enough without being involved in other people's intrigues.

Nick checked his watch.

'It's getting late. We'd best get a wriggle on if we're going to that ten-pin bowling. It looks like the rain's finished, at least. You two ready?'

He stood up. Sharon and I did too, as Christmas reluctantly jumped down from her lap.

'It's been lovely meeting you, Nancy and Arthur. The meal was wonderful. Thank you. I . . . I don't imagine we'll meet again.'

They stood as well, Arthur placing his pipe on an ash tray. The aroma was overpowering in this room, although the sash window was slightly open. Getting outside for some fresh air was an incentive to make our farewells short. However my attention was drawn to the mantelpiece with the anniversary cards displayed.

'When are these cards from?' A part of my subconscious must have realised something was not quite right. Now I could examine them more closely. The first card was very bland, yet the second was thought-provoking.

166

'Last week. We had a party with some friends and neigh — '

I was too impatient to be polite. This was too important.

'Twenty-fourth anniversary. You've been married twenty-four years? That means you had Nick before you were married.'

I stopped short of saying how hypocritical it was to insult unmarried mothers for being loose women.

Nancy's blood pressure must have shot sky-high.

'How dare you. That is absolutely unthinkable. How can you suggest that . . . a guest in our house . . . at our table? Nick was premature but we were married before . . . you know.'

Nancy was aware that Sharon was in the room.

'Excuse me. I can 'suggest it' because Nick's twenty-six. He told me so, the first day we met.'

I stared at Nick, waiting for him to agree. He stayed silent.

'That is what you said, isn't it, Nick?'

I demanded. My brain was in overdrive although logic was beginning to push another possibility to the forefront of my mind.

'Nick. I'm waiting!' I yelled impatiently, then in a more subdued tone I added, 'We're all waiting.'

Nick came up to me, taking my hands in his.

'Pamela, I can explain. It's not like that. I . . . I may have said that at the time. It was just after we met. I never thought things would go this far.'

I pulled away, dragging Sharon with me.

I was shocked. Nancy and Arthur realised at last that I'd been lied to by their son.

'Nick. Is this true? You've been seeing this woman every Saturday and Sunday, leading us to believe there was more than a friendship. I'm . . . we are very disappointed in your behaviour.'

Another bombshell. Saturday as well as Sunday! He'd told his parents he'd been with me and Sharon both days

. . . no mention of the other woman at all. This man was as dishonest as anyone could be. I was disgusted.

Furthermore I'd made a complete fool of myself accusing his parents of having a baby out of wedlock. Not that it was a problem to me — though, to them with their puritan values, I'd just accused them of being totally evil.

I turned to them abjectly.

'Nancy. Arthur. I'm so very sorry for what I said to you. It was terrible of me and — '

Arthur spoke for them both.

'We don't blame you, young lady . . . Pamela. We're just sorry that all this had to come out, especially in front of the little one. Perhaps it's better if you leave. I can drive you home.'

It was gracious of him but the way I felt, I didn't want his family to suffer any more at the sheer anger and betrayal I felt.

'That's very kind of you, Arthur. I'd prefer it if you could call us a taxi. I'll pay for the phone call.'

Nancy began to protest. 'Please let my husband drive you. It's begun raining again and — '

'The taxi's better. I'm sure you understand.'

As Arthur went to the phone, she came across to shake my hand but ended up hugging me closely. She stepped back, hanging her head. Her eyes were glistening.

'Ten minutes,' Arthur said, returning. I offered him change. He pressed it back into my hand.

Nick hadn't uttered a single word in all of this time. He appeared to be in shock at the chaos that he'd brought about.

I took hold of Sharon's hand. 'Say goodbye and thank you to Mr and Mrs Winters, please,' I told her. She did, even though she was also very upset. I could hear it in her voice. She kept staring at Nick all the time.

Nancy led us out along the hall to the front door. It was pouring outside and our raincoats plus umbrellas were in

Nick's car. There was no way I wanted to get them.

We stood with the door open, watching for the cab. Nancy left us there alone. It was about ten feet to the front gate. We shouldn't get too wet.

And if we did?

I honestly didn't care.

A taxi appeared at the top of the hill just as Nick came up behind us.

'Pamela. Don't go like this. I admit I might have been disingenuous but — ' he began to plead.

'Disingenuous, hah. Don't use your big words on me, Mr Winters. You lied about your age for one thing, as well as deceiving your parents about seeing Sharon and me on Saturdays.' I tried to keep my voice down.

The taxi pulled up in front of the gate.

'I can explain it all if you give me a ch — '

'Explain it to your blonde lady friend on the photo in your car. Sharon and I saw you with her yesterday. You should

171

have told me about her, you . . . bloody disingenuous bastard. Now leave us alone. Forever.'

Not giving him a chance to reply, I grabbed Sharon's hand and walked quickly down the steps to the gate. We were soaked in moments. I fumbled at the gate lock before opening the taxi door. I glanced at Nick, grateful he couldn't see my tears as the rain streamed down my cheeks.

'Where to, Mrs?' the driver asked.

I told him, wiped my hands across my eyes then turned for one final look as we pulled away from the curb. Nick was standing at the gate, shouting something. Between the rain and noise of the engine, I had no idea what it was.

8

It was a good thing that there was my work to throw my energies into. Whatever I had, or thought I had, with Nick was over.

Brenda arrived on Monday morning at ten for another update on progress. We had three full weeks until opening day. It sounded like a long time, but there was so much still to do. The train and track were due to arrive on site on Friday and before that, all of the infrastructure and electrics needed to be installed and tested.

The special contact I had was on holiday all week. I was confident that Bruce was going to provide the pièce de résistance to my first diorama — an event so outlandishly beautiful that Santa's Train trip would be the place to go for all Sydneysiders who were young at heart, not just children.

Not long after she arrived, Brenda asked how the weekend with Nick's family meal had gone.

'The meal was great. His parents were, too. We had a few initial problems, though it doesn't matter now. I won't be seeing Nick or them again.'

That surprised her. 'I reckoned you two were getting on OK, given that you're leaving soon. You wouldn't break it off like that without a reason. Don't tell me — he tried to push you into something intimate.'

'No. I wouldn't have minded if he did.' Brenda gave me a funny look. 'I'm a grown woman. Two people can be affectionate without doing ... you know. That was my fault, in a way. I set the boundaries but I'm not opposed to a kiss at least. Nick was a perfectly gallant man.

'Trouble was, he lied to me — and I had enough of that with Frank. My ex would tell me he was working late when all the time he was at some sleazy motel with his barely legal Sindy doll.'

'All men lie, Pamela. And women. It's human nature.'

I thought of telling her about Dave's lie regarding my train idea before deciding against it.

'He told me he was twenty-six. Turns out he's twenty-three. He's six years younger than me.'

Brenda surprised me with her own confession.

'Stan's five years younger than me. Age differences don't matter that much if you love someone. What I want to find out, Pamela, is why his age matters to you. From what you've told me you are . . . were . . . simply friends. If Nick was more than that I'd be quite flattered if I were you.'

I was somewhat surprised, firstly by her confession about Stan and then to imply that it was the age gap between Nick and me that was indicative of . . . I didn't know what.

'You misunderstand, Brenda. It was the deception. Not just with his age. He has another woman he sees.'

Brenda gave a knowing smile. 'Do I detect a note of jealousy there as well, Pamela? You were friends with Nick and now you're not. That's a shame. Not that I met him more than that one time at the barbie, but I thought he was a decent enough person — for a man, that is.'

After she left, I took a moment to consider what Brenda had said. All of those questions in the back of my mind became a jumble. Why did Nick lie about his age? Why was he so keen to show Sharon and me around Sydney? Who was this other woman and what the hell was I bothered about any of this for?

My thoughts flashed back to the terrible scene at his house. I'd relived every moment of it over and over; from sitting down in the lounge room to the moment I'd sat in the taxi as we pulled away. That final look, peering through the rain shrouded window at Nick's face as he'd stood at the gate. What had he been trying to say?

Then, in one moment of clarity, I knew.

Three words. *I love you.*

★ ★ ★

It was a good thing Dave wasn't on site for most of the week. I doubted I could deal with his smarmy comments or demands on top of the way I was feeling. Although my colleagues sensed there were problems they didn't pry or complain when I made angry or unrealistic demands. I apologised immediately, putting my unusual short temper down to a headache.

During my lunchtimes, I'd wander aimlessly around the part of Waratah World that had been opened three years before, often standing at the Waterfall Fountain where the carol singers from Nick's church would be in two weeks' time. There was no possibility of joining them in practice or on the Thursday night performances leading up to

Christmas itself. After all, Nick would be there.

At nights, Sharon was much more subdued. I'd discussed what had happened, deciding, as usual, to explain the truth about why I was angry. She didn't understand and, in retrospect, neither did I. I felt that he'd broken our relationship which had been built on trust.

As she slept, I sat up trying to resolve my feelings. I should have been packing or planning to leave Australia; I simply didn't have the energy.

It was Thursday evening when I arrived home to collect Sharon that Mrs de Luca told me that a telegram had been delivered earlier.

Immediately, I felt sick. Telegrams were never good news. Were my parents ill?

I opened it then and there. Sharon was still watching that *Skippy* programme on the telly.

'Bad news?' Mrs de Luca enquired.

'Not to me personally. My grandmother has passed away. I haven't seen her since ... I guess since the late 1940s, twenty years ago. She and my family were never close, although lately there has been a thawing, I gather. I'm surprised the news warranted a telegram. Granny Balitsky, I used to call her. Her father was Polish.'

I dropped the telegram into my handbag and dismissed her from my thoughts.

★　★　★

That night I awoke in a cold sweat. I didn't usually have nightmares, though my parents told me that I often did as a child, waking screaming and crying loudly enough to disturb our neighbours.

Granny Balitsky was in the one I'd just had. I was a little girl again and she was yelling at me for dirtying my dress while playing. However it was more than a rebuke; it was blazing eyes, raising her hands, terrifying anger. I was cowering in a corner and tried to run

179

past her but she was faster. I felt her grab my arm, her sharp nails digging into my flesh, dragging me off the floor. It was the way she stared at me through her glasses ... I knew what she was going to do next; something so dreadful that it shocked me awake, my heart pounding in my chest.

I went for some water, firstly splashing some on my face in the bathroom. The nightmare was almost forgotten, though I did recall that feeling.

Staring at the face in the mirror, I heard myself say softly, 'I'm not sorry that you're dead, Granny. Not sorry at all.'

★   ★   ★

On the morning of Friday I kept feeling guilty at harbouring such ungracious thoughts. My granny had cared for me during a year or so at the height of bombing during the war. I was too young to remember much of my time

180

down there in her Herefordshire farm. I could recall bits about the farm but not her. As for that nightmare; why would my subconscious weave such a horrid vision of her? Perhaps I should ask my mum about her in my next letter. After all, Granny was her mother.

It was the Train arrival day with trucks ferrying in the engine, carriages and track. Obviously the priority was laying the track, though my design team needed to make a start on the festive theme and sign-writing on the rolling stock. The plan was in place, and so was Dave, pretending he was in charge. Most of the team suspected the truth about whose idea it was. I'd never told them but when you get vague answers to questions from the bloke supposedly in charge and detailed plans and timetables from the dogsbody, the truth hadn't been too hard to guess.

I headed home, feeling surprisingly sad that Sharon and I weren't going somewhere special on Sunday. It had only been a few weeks that we'd gone out with Nick, yet it seemed longer. Sharon was still upset about the argument on Sunday and I didn't blame her. It could have been handled much more sensitively by me. Antagonism and accusations weren't normally the way I dealt with conflict situations.

Saturday found me heading down to the travel agents ready to pay the balance for our flights. It was earlier than the deadline, yet there was no reason to delay. I had a cheque made out ready to pay Darleen at the agency.

I'd left Sharon with Mrs de Luca. It wouldn't have been much fun for her sitting through all the paperwork. Purchasing a treat would be all she wanted from the shops in any case.

On the way, I called into the camera shop where I'd left two films for processing. All through the construction of the train set, I'd taken photographs for my records. They were in colour. In the shop, the assistant handed me the envelopes with the prints and negatives. I'd paid for the larger seven by five-inch prints on glossy paper.

'Can you check they're yours, please, Mrs Grant? Can't have you wandering off with someone else's birthday piccies, can we?'

I should have realised that some would be of our times with Nick. The first ones were of the koala park, mainly of Sharon feeding the kangaroos or wallabies as well as her cuddling a koala. Then there was the one of Nick and the emu. I smiled, before putting them back in the envelope.

Dear, sweet Nick. Why did you have to lie?

It was a windy day, although warm enough for short sleeves. A part of me was watching for Nick across the street in those bright green shorts of his. I hated the fact that he'd become so much a part of our lives. It was the very thing that I wanted to avoid, so close to us leaving.

Blossom was dancing through the air as the breezes rose and ebbed, like the petals at the Gardens in Sydney. A car drove through a puddle from last night's storm, splashing my legs with cold water. For an instant I was back at Lawson, Nick pulling me from the mountain stream.

I forced myself from my daydreams. Time to visit Darleen before my resolve weakened.

*   *   *

Talk about red tape. I'd come prepared with all the forms that were required.

It's not as though I'm buying a house, I thought.

Fair enough, they wanted my passport; two years since the Australian entry stamp had been placed on one of the pages. But why all the rest? A declaration from my bank that I had no hire-purchase agreements that I might default on, our birth certificates and some other documentation to clarify that I was divorced, although I'd had our surnames altered on the passports already.

'Now Pamela. Let's sort out your daughter's forms. I've seen her passport. What I need now is permission to take Sharon out of Australia.'

I leafed through the papers in the manila envelope that I'd brought and handed some stapled pages across the desk.

Darleen flicked through. 'Sorry. It's not here.'

I leaned across to check. 'But it is. That's the custody agreement, signed and sealed by the court. It gives me sole custody of Sharon.'

Darleen chewed her lip. 'It's not enough, I'm afraid. We require form BZ 652, signed by Mr . . . ' she checked her notes, 'Mr Francis Greenstreet, acknowledging that he gives permission for your daughter to leave Australia permanently.' She put the paperwork down to face me.

'No. That can't be right. I have custody.'

This was not going well.

'Under Australian law, the rights of the father must be respected in these matters. Custody is one thing but the law says that he must — '

'Damn it, Darleen. Even if I accepted what you're telling me, there is no possible way I can get him to sign that bloody form.' My tone, raised voice and use of a swear word quite acceptable from men, was attracting disapproving attention from other staff and clientèle.

'Please calm down, Mrs Grant. I don't make the rules. However you will not be permitted to board any plane until this form is signed.' With an effort I sat back, relaxing my belligerent stance. 'Why is it that you foresee a problem?'

I sighed and took a deep breath.

'I have no idea where Frank is. I assume he's still in the country, maybe in Brisbane, but who knows? That's why I can't get a signature. What happens in that case?'

'I . . . I don't know. Can I ask my boss? It's never happened before.'

Darleen summoned her manager, an older man with a permanent smile and a silvery-grey moustache. He smelled of garlic.

'What seems to be the problem here, Darleen?'

The young woman explained. The manager's permanent smile faded. He was sitting next to Darleen when he addressed me.

'As far as I understand these regulations, Mrs . . . Mrs Grant, it will be necessary for the Government department concerned to advertise in newspapers, requesting that your ex-husband, Mr Greenstreet, contact them to give permission. If they hear nothing after a given period of time then they assume they've done all they could to comply with the law and you'll then be given dispensation to leave Australia with your child.'

I was becoming even more despondent and impatient by this point.

'Exactly how long is this period of time?'

I was under no illusion that they'd find Frank. He was not a reliable man, always searching for the next excuse for an easy life without responsibilities. It had taken me too long to realise that. Now I knew him only too well.

The manager was searching through a thick book of regulations.

'Please bear with me, Mrs Grant. Ah here it is . . . 'period of time' . . . 'not less than two hundred days'. Yes, that's right, two — '

'What? Over six months? You're telling me that I'm stuck here for six bloody months waiting for my ex-husband to sign a paper saying it's all right for my daughter to leave! The toe-rag has had nothing to do with her, yet now his say-so is more important than mine?'

'I'm afraid so, Mrs Grant. And please compose yourself. There's nothing to stop *you* leaving,' said the officious little man.

'You can't be serious, Mr whoever-you-are. I can leave, and do what with

Sharon? Leave her in Australia? With my missing husband, perhaps? Or in your office, sitting in that corner over there? And what — get on with my life over in England then come back in six months?'

It was fortunate that the other people had left. One of the other staff members, a woman, came up to us.

'Mrs Grant — ' the manager began defensively.

'Shut up, Harold. I'll handle this. Mrs Grant is very upset and you're not helping with your insensitive suggestions. Make yourself useful. Get us two cups of tea, milk and sugar. Now.'

I waited until he'd left before bursting into tears. The woman and Darleen both came round to comfort me, finally leading me to an office at the rear of the shop. Darleen returned to deal with a new customer. The woman gave me a clean hanky before taking the tea from the very contrite man and closing the door on him. I took a sip from my cup. It was too sweet, but it helped.

'My hubby can be an unfeeling so-and-so at times. He means well but he has no understanding of what he's put you through. I'm sorry for that.'

I dried my eyes and took a deep breath. Just another setback to my life and Sharon's. It wasn't the end of the world.

'Thank you for that.' It was genuine. Right now I needed all the help and support I could get, and this kindly lady was at least ready to listen.

'Mrs Grant — Pamela, if I may — these regulations favouring the rights of men, of fathers, are archaic and wrong. I know that and so do you. However until the law changes, we must comply with it. We need to set things in motion to allow you to leave Australia as soon as you can. I personally will do all I can to guide you through what's required. It's not part of my job as a travel agent but it is my job as a woman. Is that acceptable?'

I gave her a wan smile and dabbed my eyes.

'Right. Thank you. Where do we begin?'

9

By the time I left at twelve-thirty, I'd regained a sense of purpose. Jennifer, the co-owner, had set things in motion to comply with the archaic rules.

Obviously all Government offices were closed on Saturdays but the newspaper offices for placing the particular ads weren't. It transpired I'd have to pay for the advertisements; that was the only way past the impasse.

As Mum used to say to me, 'Life's unfair, Pamela. You just hitch up your knickers and get on with it.' This was one of those times.

I had my deposit back. There was no possibility of spending this Christmas in England. My job was another matter. The temporary contract finished in a month, so that was a worry. It was moments like this that I felt so alone.

Mrs de Luca was lovely yet she had

her own concerns, missing her family. *If only Nick was here to talk to*, I thought, wistfully . . . but that boat had sailed. Remembering the confrontation last Sunday, the boat had probably sunk as well.

That's why I was surprised to see a car like Nick's parents' blue Valiant pulling away when I turned the corner of our street. It was a steep hill and my feet were killing me from the new stilettos that I'd stupidly decided to wear.

Sharon rushed up to me as soon as I opened Mrs de Luca's back door. It was an informal arrangement that I simply knocked and went in. I realised I'd forgotten her chocolate, though she didn't seem bothered. She had the white kitten held gently in her hands.

We had a quick catch-up before she went off again, this time into the garden. That suited me. I needed to talk to my landlady.

After explaining the new predicament

I was in, she immediately put my mind at rest.

'You are welcome to stay here as long as you wish, Pamela; you and the little one. She is a joy to have here, so well behaved.'

I hugged her warmly. Then I remembered.

'Was somebody just here?'

'Oh yes. I forgot. My memory these days. It was the parents of your Nick. They bring the raincoats and other items you leave on Sunday. Nancy think it better for them to come, rather than your young man. He misses you and Sharon.'

That was a lot of information to take in.

'How long were they here?'

'About an hour. Had tea and cake. Arthur and Sharon play Snakes and Ladders. Nancy and me have a good woman to woman talk. They both seem very kind.'

I wasn't sure about this. It was pleasing that there seemed to be no hard feelings about me or my inexcusable accusations. Even so, to spend an hour here when they were ostensibly simply returning some cheap clothing, was unexpected.

'Did they come to see me?'

'Not especially. They knock on my door, ask if you are home, seem relieved you are not. I believe they think it too soon to speak to you in person and no, they were not prying. We spend most time talking about our children.' Then she slapped her hand gently against her forehead.

'Porca miseria! I almost forget, Pamela. The letters.' She gave me two envelopes, one of which was addressed to Nick and already opened. On the front of the other was a note in red Biro, *Open me first*.

I had no secrets from my landlady. Moreover, I'd decided to invite her to ours for lunch. I needed some company more today than I could remember.

Sitting down, I quickly read the one addressed to me. It was from Nick. I paraphrased it for her.

'He starts off by apologising about the age thing. He lied to start with at the barbecue so that I didn't send him away because he was too young. And then, after we became closer, he could never admit to being so dishonest. That's fair enough. Not that I can understand why he wanted to go out with someone older, but it shouldn't matter. We were simply friends after all.'

Mrs de Luca listened patiently.

'It seems he wants to be more than friends though, Pamela. Despite knowing you leaving soon. Maybe he hopes you change your mind and stay with him?'

I hadn't considered that. How utterly dense he must have been to think I'd alter our future plans because of a few weeks with a new man in our lives. Then I recalled his final frantic words last Sunday. *I love you.*

Surely not, I thought. It sounded incomprehensible to me, but men in general and Nick in particular were a strange species.

'You don't think he fell in love with me the minute he met me, do you? After all, he knew nothing about me at all. It's not logical.'

Mrs D burst into laughter.

'Love isn't logical, Pamela. Love is ruled by the heart. You realise that. You have heard perhaps of love at first sight? No?'

'But I don't love him.'

Mrs D gave me one of those enigmatic stares of hers. I opened his letter once more.

'Anyway, he hopes that Sharon and I will continue with the choir and Christmas carols. Although he'll be there he promises to stay out of our way. He won't even speak if we don't want.'

'Will you? Go to the choir?'

I considered that. After all, it was fun and we seemed destined to be here for Christmas.

'Yes. I can't see any reason why not.

One more practice night, then we start at the shopping centre on the fourteenth.'

'That's a good decision. Sharon has been practising by herself. She knows most of the words by heart. What about the other letter?'

I looked at the return name and address. It was from Gwen.

'She's the lady who Nick saved when she collapsed on the Manly ferry,' I explained. 'She took a photo of the three of us on the boat. Said we made a lovely family.'

Mrs de Luca looked shocked. She went out to the kitchen, returning with a handful of photos.

'I forgot again. We were looking at these photos. Nick sent them. I think I saw the one you just mentioned . . . ah yes, here it is.'

She passed me the pictures. The picture from the ferry was on top. It evoked fond memories of that first date with Nick. *Date?* I meant day. I put the photos down, time enough to examine

Nick's and mine later. Sharon would love them.

'Let's read her letter. Nick said in his that this Gwen lady was very grateful for saving her life and this letter has an invitation. He can't go, however he thought Sharon and I might be interested.'

Mrs de Luca commented that this was a kind gesture on his part. After all, the letter was addressed to him alone.

I had to agree. Had it not been for his lies, who knows what might have happened between us.

We read the letter together.

'Oh my,' I said at the end. 'Sharon loves that show. Do you watch it with her?'

'I didn't to begin with, but now I'm a big fan. Sharon would love to visit where they make the show. You would too, Pamela. It's a shame that you're at work when it's on telly. What do you think? Will you accept her invitation?'

A chance to see a real live Australian movie star?

'Of course. I'll phone her later. Right now, shall we go and have lunch?'

It had been the perfect boost to the day after this morning's devastating news. I couldn't wait to tell Sharon about our upcoming visit to where they filmed *Skippy, The Bush Kangaroo*.

★ ★ ★

After lunch at my flat, we enjoyed some time perusing the photos before I told Sharon about our special trip. My winsome girl was ecstatic. I didn't realise how much she adored the show. We went out together to the phone box to phone the kind lady. Gwen was very friendly, assuring us it would be no trouble at all to visit any time in the next two weeks. After that, the set was closed over the holiday period.

'Would Tuesday week suit you, Gwen?' I asked her. It was the best option for me work-wise. It would also mean another day off, something I had no doubt that Dave would object to.

'Tuesday the twelfth? Great. Give me your address and I'll have a driver pick you up. Eight o'clock, not too early. It'll be a full day with lunch at the Park.'

'The Park?' I asked, stupidly.

'Where Skippy lives,' Sharon yelled. Gwen could hear her enthusiasm.

'Oh.' I could see I needed to do some research before we went. I didn't want to appear totally ignorant on the day.

★　★　★

Monday would be a special day for both me and the Train. The Snowman was coming. Bruce Graham was an engineer who managed a blossoming company that specialised in air conditioning and refrigeration. I'd met him socially a year before and we'd worked successfully on two projects since then.

I had a very special task for him this time. His business was expanding and was now moving into domestic cooling as well as the larger industrial and commercial.

Before he arrived, though, I wandered down to the local bookshop that was near the main entrance. There were dozens of books of all types about Australia's celebrity kangaroo ranging from comics to annuals and colouring books.

I bought a few for Sharon, conscious that her Christmas stocking would now have to be stuffed with Australian gifts. In a way, it would be better. I could take my time choosing them rather than a last-minute buying spree in Manchester. My delayed departure from Australia did have compensations; every cloud, and all that.

There were also some books for me. I had a week to . . . well, not become an expert on Skippy but at least find out enough to get by. I even bought an autograph book for Sharon to get the kangaroo's signature. It seemed he could do everything else apart from talking, so I figured a signature wasn't out of the question.

'Looks like you're a Skippy admirer,

Miss,' said the bubbly shop assistant.

'Not yet. My daughter and I will be guests where it's filmed. I just wanted to find out what all the fuss is about.'

'You are one lucky lady. I really hope you have a super-duper day. Can you come back and tell me about it after you've been?'

'Certainly. I'm working down at the new extension on Santa's Train so it's handy.'

As I walked back to work, I felt a touch guilty. It was Nick who deserved the special day out.

Bruce arrived a few minutes later. He was one of those larger-than-life blokes, six foot two and with a jet black Peter Wyngarde moustache to match his flowing ebony locks. A chunky gold chain was clearly visible under his epaulette shoulder shirt. We greeted one another warmly.

'G'day, Pamela. Good to hear from you. Reckoned you might have disappeared back to Pommieland without saying hoo-roo to yer best mate.'

'No chance of that, Brucie. Besides. I'm stuck here for awhile yet.'

I explained the situation and he had a few words to say about the drongos and no-hopers in Government too.

'Reckon it's the same back in England. That Guy Fawkes bloke might have had the right idea. Isn't it your Bonfire Night tomorrow?' he reminded me. 'My birthday, Guy Fawkes Day and Melbourne Cup Day all together. Me mum was going to name me Guy. Either that or the horse that won the Cup. Glad she settled on Bruce.'

I wished him a happy birthday in advance before reminiscing briefly about Bonfire Night with parkin cake and treacle toffee. Being upside down, Australia had their firework night on Commonwealth Day six months earlier. They called it Cracker Night.

I decided to make treacle toffee that night with Sharon, although we wouldn't have any fireworks.

'Tell you what, Brucie. I'll prepare some traditional bonfire goodies and bring them in tomorrow for you and the family. Assuming you agree to work here, of course. How many children now?' He was the ultimate family man.

'Still only four but number five's on the way. I'm hoping for a boy this time. All those girls plus the cook; a bloke can feel outnumbered at times.'

He doted on them all despite what he might say. Eventually we moved past the small talk.

'No sweat. Anyway, what's on yer mind here, Pamela?'

I took him on the guided tour. The rails were being laid but there was room to bypass the workmen. We stopped at the town scene with the carollers.

'This is it, Brucie. First taste of the North Pole.'

He examined the snow-clad houses with their steep roofs and the painted fir trees nestled on the mountain range in the background.

'Let me guess. Yer want a blast of cold air as the train exits the tunnel.' He was already weighing up the logistics of fitting air conditioning pipes and vents to the starry night sky ceiling. 'After all, that's why I'm here. Right?'

'Sort of. However I want more than that, my friend. I want . . . snow.'

He spun around to stare me in the eyes. I wasn't smiling or laughing so he eventually concluded, 'Fair dinkum? Ye're not joking. Snow? In here . . . during an Aussie summer? I know folks call me the snowman but — '

'Are you telling me you can't do it? Shame. I thought with your reputation . . . '

'Hold on, Pamela. Didn't say I couldn't do it. Just might give me a few more grey hairs. Tell me you don't want a snowstorm.'

'I don't. Just proper snow from the sky. Think about the magic of it, Bruce.' Then I gave him the sweetener, already OK'd with Brenda and the centre manager. 'Moreover, I've arranged two months free rent for a booth outside the exhibit. You are moving into household air conditioning, aren't you?'

I could see the dollar signs in his eyes. Perfect advertising, travelling on Santa's Train, plus a prime-location booth in Waratah World. All those parents feeling the cool air on the Train then realising they could have that in their home every summer from now on.

'Now, Bruce. Talk to me. Can we have it snowing here in two weeks?'

★ ★ ★

Thursday was the last rehearsal before the carol singers were to perform at the centre. Given our new situation, I'd decided to accept Nick's offer. He kept his distance from us exactly as he'd promised. As Sharon wanted to speak to him, I let her. She told him where she and I were going with Gwen and Nick, being Nick, feigned surprise to hear her news.

Once we completed our practice the general consensus was that we sounded pretty darn good; not professional standard mind you, but what we lacked in ability we made up for in enthusiasm. Just to add that special touch, we agreed on a dress code. At least we'd look like a group, the guys wearing white shirts with dark slacks and us ladies in dark skirts or slacks plus white blouses.

It was me who approached Nick as we made ready to leave the church. It was awkward for both of us I guessed, however I wanted to thank him for the photos and Gwen's letter. I also told him about the delay in getting permission to take Sharon back to the UK.

'Is there no possibility that we can get together again, Pamela? I thought we had a good relationship and we get on so well.'

'Nick. You're a lovely person but I realise you want more from our relationship than I'm prepared to give. I'm assuming that you did actually say that you loved me the other day?'

He nodded, sheepishly.

'I do like you but I'm not comfortable with the age difference. Nick — you're so young. You're much better off with someone your own age . . . or younger. It's the way things are between men and women. Thinking about it, I can forgive you for telling those porkies about your age. I overreacted the other day at your home. But that doesn't explain that other woman Sharon and I saw you with that Saturday. You obviously care about her. Care to explain?'

He shifted uncomfortably on his feet. The others had left and the three of us were standing outside the church alone. Suddenly the outside lights went off, causing me to realise how dark it was apart from the street lamps thirty yards away. I fumbled in my bag for my emergency torch.

'You all right, Pamela? You're shaking.'

Nick was concerned.

'Afraid of the dark,' I confessed, slowing my breathing. I avoided shining the torch at Nick's eyes. The shadows made him look a little terrifying.

'Like spiders, then?'

'No. Much, much worse. A childhood phobia. I'm OK if it's not pitch black. Don't avoid the subject. Who's your mystery woman, Nick?'

'I can't tell you, Pamela. A promise I made. Can't you trust me when I tell you that I love only you and she has nothing to do with my feelings for you?' He reached for my hand. I stepped away.

'My first husband had another woman in his life. I trusted him and he betrayed that trust. You have your reasons for not telling me, I suppose, but until you explain, I can't let myself have feelings for you . . . ever. And, given the way you feel about me, I can't see a future for us, even as friends. I'm sorry, Nick. I really do like you. Goodbye.'

It hurt to take Sharon's hand, turn away and leave him.

★　★　★

We had a quiet weekend, spending some time listening to the Remembrance Sunday Service on the radio. I felt a kinship with my dad, who would be marching with his naval comrades and observing the traditional silence. My grandmother, the one who had just passed away, had lost her son during the war.

Monday came. We had a week until the Train began running. It was all checked out and waiting on the track with its carriages. The art team had it painted up a treat, with *Santa's Train* emblazoned on the engine. Each carriage had a different reindeer's name painted on both sides.

Brenda was back from her holidays and eager to see progress. Bruce was busy with his industrial refrigeration unit set well away from the train. The theory was that the cool air under pressure would precipitate snow as the pressure was released.

'Looking good, Pamela. HJ has OK'd a small party Wednesday evening after knock-off time. Nibbles plus drinks. Any preference for spirits?'

'I don't drink, Brenda. Can't handle spirits at all. Knocks me out big time. I'll stick with one shandy and then some pineapple juice.'

'Each to their own. You appear to have done a superb job with Dave's design. It'll be a shame to lose you from the team — and as a friend — when you go.'

'Actually I wanted to discuss my contract with you. There have been some . . . developments.' I took her back to the office for some privacy.

Once I'd explained the situation about Sharon needing permission to leave and that I'd be in Australia for the foreseeable, she told me that she'd discuss my future with HJ. She was hopeful that I could extend my employment with them. I was so relieved.

'I'll let you know tomorrow.' It was already late in the day.

'I'm off Tuesday, remember.'

'Oh yes, I forgot. I must say that

Dave wasn't happy with you taking more time off so close to finishing his Train. We have a meeting with HJ tomorrow. He expected you to be there to explain the finer points. Where are you off to anyway?'

'Taking Sharon to meet Skippy.'

'Oh — the zoo. You could have gone there any time, Pamela.'

I became defensive. 'Not the zoo, Brenda. We're going to the set where they film *Skippy*. They're sending a car to pick us up and we're having lunch with the actors — '

'If you say so, Pamela. Dave did suggest you had delusions of grandeur sometimes.'

I stared at the woman who I'd regarded as a friend . . . until now. She didn't believe me!

'Did he just? Perhaps you should know the truth about your precious Dave. The idea for Santa's Train? It was all mine. He stole it.'

Now it was Brenda who stared at me, her mouth open in shock.

10

Telling Brenda had been an impulse thing. I was suddenly concerned about Dave's reaction if he found out.

'Pamela. Are you telling me that this Santa's Train concept was your idea from the start?'

Something in Brenda's tone made me uneasy.

'Y . . . yeah. I told him, prepared the brief for HJ and the next thing I find out the little bastard has claimed it was his brainwave all along.'

'Pamela. Language, please.'

'Well, he is. Even threatened me if I told anyone. He — '

'Be quiet, Pamela. It's one thing to accuse your boss of being dishonest but I cannot allow you to call him such horrid names. He warned HJ and I that you might claim it was your vision, though I refused to believe

214

you'd stoop so low.'

She was defending Dave! I couldn't believe it. Dave had poisoned her opinion.

'Brenda — I — '

'Enough. If you weren't already leaving in a few weeks, I'd tell HJ what you've just said. You'd be out on your ear, quick smart. As it is, I'll say nothing now but if I hear any more slanderous claims, I'll make sure you're sacked.'

'But . . . I thought we were friends.' I began to sob.

'Dry your tears, you hussy. Whatever we were, is finished. I'm disgusted with you. Now, get out of my sight.'

I left her and made my way to the temporary ladies where I could cry without being observed. I was devastated. Dave had foreseen that I might tell and had set me up good and proper. He was my superior. Naturally they'd believe him over me. How could I have been so utterly naïve?

Everything was going wrong with my

life, yet the worst thing was that none of it was my fault. I'd stood up for myself to Nick and now Brenda though neither situation had worked out well.

Despite feeling let down by Brenda, I didn't blame her. It seemed Dave was a master manipulator of people and she was taken in by his subterfuge just as I had been. Nevertheless it hurt. After Brenda had departed for the day, Dave had come to ask me some details about costs and other construction related details that he needed for the next day. I looked at my watch.

'Sorry boss. It's knock-off time. I'll see you Wednesday.'

There was no possibility that I'd let him know he'd got under my skin again. Any thoughts of not taking Sharon tomorrow were also swept aside. My mother's words went through my mind again. *Get on with it, girl.*

No, tomorrow was going to be awesome. I might not have a job to come back to, but I'd deal with that later.

Unfortunately that resolve was tested when I opened another aerogramme from home. It was from my sister and was in reply to one I'd sent a few weeks earlier.

This Nick person sounds like he has you smitten, Pamela. Nick this and Nick that, he's so good with Sharon etc. Who would have thought you'd fall in love with a colonial?

Surely I hadn't been that effusive in my letter. Or maybe I had been, without realising it. In any case, I had tea to prepare plus find and iron some clothes to wear tomorrow. It was going to be a special day, and no amount of feeling miffed was going to spoil our day out.

Besides I still had some serious study to do if I was going to become au fait with Skippy and his friends.

* * *

We rose at the crack of dawn to get ready. Neither of us could sleep anyway because of the excitement. I'd dressed Sharon in her prettiest frock, sky-blue with a white bodice and collar. I chose a red shift dress with a white bow and matching red shoes, bracelet and handbag. After much debate, I opted to leave the stilettos at home as we were apparently walking around the outdoor set at Waratah National Park.

Mrs de Luca came out with us to wait on the street. It was quite still, which suited me as I'd chosen to wear a wide-brim straw hat. When the car arrived we were all very impressed. It was one of those big American cars with shiny chrome everywhere. It pulled up just ahead of where we were standing; a Chevrolet Impala.

Gwen stepped out from the passenger door. She seemed to have lost a little weight from her face since we'd spoken to her on the ferry. That was understandable, given the health problems she had.

Once we'd greeted one another warmly, I asked her how she was.

'Taking things easier, Pamela. It made me realise there's more to life than work. It is hard to let go but my family are keeping an eye on me. You'll meet my son later.'

She knelt down to speak to Sharon.

'Are you excited to see Skippy?' she asked.

'Oh yes, Mrs Pattison. I have my autograph book. See? And I've been practising my Skippy jump.' She gave us a demonstration.

Gwen laughed. 'That is impressive, Sharon. I reckon Skippy will be very jealous.'

The driver came around to open our doors.

'This is Matt, my man Friday. He's my driver and assistant but mainly he's my friend. We've been together . . . oh, how long now, Matt?'

'Twelve years, Gwen. Shall we go now? The traffic over the Bridge is usually heavy at this time and you all have a busy day.'

Sharon and I made a move to get

into the back seat. The car was huge.

'No. Miss Sharon is riding up front with me and you two ladies will be in the back. If that's OK, of course.'

Sharon's eyes were wide open.

'Can I . . . I mean, may I, Mummy? Please?'

I grinned before a fleeting memory of Brenda's anger from yesterday upset me for a moment. Sharon was waiting, almost bursting with anticipation. The exuberance of youth.

'Of course you may.' I suspected that Gwen wanted a quiet word with me.

Once in, I made a move to open the window. The morning was warming up quickly. There was no handle.

'Electric windows,' explained Gwen. 'Leave them up. Air conditioning. Much more civilised.'

'In a car? Wow. And I suppose that's a refrigerated bar in there.' I indicated a console.

'No, that's my mobile office. I have a two-way radio. The bar's over here. Who'd like a cold drink?'

'Just a soft drink or fruit juice for us, please.'

'Too early in the day for me to have anything else. In any case, between my doctor and Matt here, I'm on the wagon every day now.'

She passed the drinks around as we turned onto Parramatta Road. Everyone seemed to be looking at us in the flash car. I felt like royalty.

Gwen lowered her voice. 'It's obvious that you've got things on your mind, Pamela. Over the years I've learned to read people very well, if I do say so. I owe Nick my life, Pamela. He's a decent bloke. If you feel like talking I'm a good listener.'

'Appreciate the offer, Gwen. It's not Nick that I'm upset about. Problems at work.'

After some gentle encouragement to open up, I did. Gwen was a great confidante. Before I knew it we were on the Bridge heading towards the northern suburbs. A train passed by, scant feet from us. I found myself staring at the passengers, most of whom were watching us.

Gwen was digesting all that I'd told her. She took another sip of her drink.

'I've heard of this Santa's Train Christmas ride. It was on the telly last night. An ad. Did you watch it?'

'No telly, I'm afraid. I've never seen *Skippy* either, though Sharon loves it. She sings the song all the time.' I winced, unconsciously.

Gwen gave a little chuckle. 'The song is one you can't get out of your head. That's for sure.'

'Don't get me wrong. I've been reading up about it. Sounds like super entertainment for all the family. I'd like to watch it but . . . '

'The time of the day? You do realise we're making a film for the theatres. Plus there's a new device coming out where you can record television on a tape and play it back later.'

I was surprised. Technology was really galloping ahead. 'Like a cassette recorder, or those old tape recorders

222

they used for speech or music? That would be wonderful. You could keep your favourite shows and watch them whenever you wanted.' My mind was full of thoughts for the future. First thing, once we had our house in England, I intended to rent a telly, maybe one of those new colour ones.

We'd become distracted.

'Pamela. I'll be honest. If you're the person who visualised this Train ride, including the snow and all the other scenes you've told me about, then I'm sure we can find a position in set design for you. Our company is involved with other shows apart from *Skippy*, or hadn't you realised?'

I confessed my ignorance. Nevertheless, her offer of a position put my mind at rest. I thanked Gwen and began to relax. It was going to be a great day out.

Gwen sensed my attitude change. 'Special show for Skippy, Sharon,' she told my daughter. 'We're making our Christmas episode today.'

'But it's not Christmas yet,' Sharon

replied, a little confused.

I chose to step in. 'Sweetheart. You know that photo on the ferry that Mrs Pattison took of Nick, me and you?'

'Yes.'

'But we only saw the photo the other day. Television is like that. They take the photos one day and show them on another, maybe weeks afterwards.' Sharon nodded.

Gwen leaned forward. 'What the cameraman takes today will be shown on Christmas Day all over Australia.'

Sharon was now wondering about the show.

'Will Skippy meet Santa Claus? Or Rudolph? Maybe he'll save Santa when his sleigh is broke down?'

'I can see you've got a very good imagination, Sharon. Perhaps you'll be a writer.'

'Thank you, Mrs Pattison. I love reading and making up stories.' She thought about what she'd heard before asking, 'Mummy, what's 'magination' mean?'

★ ★ ★

Gwen did try and explain her company's role in television production but it was over my head. I'd seen the terms producer and director on film credits at the Saturday double-features, though I never understood what they did. As for a gaffer or a best boy, I shuddered to think about them.

We arrived at the studios soon afterwards. They weren't huge like the ones I'd seen in movies, but it was exciting. Then Gwen introduced us to the crew on a set I recognised from the books I'd bought. It was the ranger's home and office.

Sharon seemed disappointed and bored but suddenly came alive when a handler brought a kangaroo on set, followed by the actor who played Sonny. He was older than Sharon but went out of his way to make her feel welcome.

The following three hours were enthralling. Everyone was so welcoming, with Gwen taking pains to show us around and watch some indoor scenes being filmed. '*Skippy* is being shown in England. We've sold it to quite a few overseas countries. The whole world appears to be fascinated by Australia and our unique wildlife.'

'I've never seen how they make a telly show before. There are loads of people involved.'

Gwen leaned over to whisper to me. 'Loads of Skippys too. We have nine of them, trained to do different tasks. Best not to tell Sharon, though. Shattering kiddies' dreams isn't good, is it?'

I don't think she meant anything by it, though I immediately thought of a conversation with Sharon before Nick and I had our disagreement.

'Do you think Nick would marry you, Mummy? Then he could be my daddy.'

She'd clearly become attached to him. Maybe she believed in love at first sight too — yet I could not believe I'd ever suggested I had romantic feelings for Nick. Especially in front of Sharon.

'Take a break, everyone,' the director

said. 'Lunch, then onto the coach at one-thirty.'

'The coach?' I said.

Gwen stood, ushering us to the canteen to join everyone for a meal. 'We take everyone to location on a specially-equipped coach and whatever cameras and other equipment we need in a truck. We're headed out to shoot the final scenes on location at — '

'At Waratah National Park,' Sharon said on cue. She'd been listening to conversations, it seemed. Maybe Sonny had told her . . . or Skippy?

*　　*　　*

Out in the bush, they seemed to take ages setting up each shot. There were a number of takes as well. Shooting a show outdoors had its own special list of problems.

'How was that scene?' said the director after shouting 'Cut'.'

The cameraman gave it the thumbs-up, as did others, including the person checking the script.

'No good,' shouted the guy with earphones on working with the sound recording machine. 'Kookaburra laughed over Sonny's lines.'

The director glared at the bird above our heads.

'Bloody bird,' he said, before realising Sharon was there. 'Sorry, Pamela.'

'It's OK,' I replied. 'She's heard worse.' It seemed that we couldn't escape some of the Australianisms so I needed to have 'one of those talks' with my daughter. Possibly another one about boys and girls, too. I'd grown up being told that babies come from cabbage patches; no way would my daughter be fed such rubbish.

'Right. Let's do that scene again. And you,' he said to the kingfisher up above. 'Shut your flaming beak. Please.'

Eventually they were ready to shoot the last scene, which involved the whole cast standing outside Ranger Headquarters with Skippy. The Park's helicopter was parked nearby. As for

Skippy, she was wearing a Santa hat with her ears sticking through specially cut holes.

'OK, everyone. This is the last scene of the Christmas episode. Clancy's aunt and cousin are arriving from England, especially to celebrate Christmas Day with her and her friends. Hold on, where are the two extras?'

'They're not coming, boss. The car broke down. They just phoned.'

I had a horrible premonition at those words, especially since the entire cast and crew were smirking.

The director checked his watch. 'It's too late to hire someone else. They'll take forever getting here. Where can we find someone to play Aunt Judy and her daughter Polly?'

I felt like I was on the top of a roller-coaster knowing what was going to happen next but unable to change the future. We'd been set up.

'How old is the girl supposed to be?' said Sonny, on cue.

The director glanced at the script.

'Four. Almost five. And it says here she must have brown hair like her mother's.'

By this time, Sharon was looking at the group of people who had turned to us.

'That's the same age as Sharon. And she has brown hair also,' said Clancy. 'You don't suppose Sharon and Pamela could help us out by pretending to be my cousin and auntie?'

'Let's ask them.'

Sharon was on her feet, sensing what he was about to do. She could hardly contain herself.

I mouthed a quiet *thank you* to Gwen, who was grinning away on the sidelines. It seemed as though Sharon and I were to become actors.

We were taken to wardrobe and make-up, then given our special copies of scripts signed by the cast and crew. Even Skippy had put her paw print on them. The director explained what we must do. There were no words, only actions, arriving in a Jeep then getting out and hugging Clancy before shaking paws with the star of the show.

The rehearsals went well, but there was another surprise lined up — one that shocked even me.

'You know what would make this a really special ending to our Christmas show? Instead of the Jeep, why not have them arrive by helicopter?'

Sharon's eyes couldn't open any wider. I supposed she'd seen the helicopter on the television, taking off and landing.

The next ten minutes were wonderful for the both of us. We actually flew up in the helicopter, although it was just a few feet. Landing, then following our script was wonderful. I prayed I didn't screw it up by looking at the camera. Sharon, on the other hand, was a natural actress.

It was the perfect end to a perfect day. Before we said our goodbyes to the people there plus Skippy, we were given lots of photos of us taken throughout the day while we weren't watching.

During the ride home, Sharon sat in

the back with me. It had been an exhausting day so she was soon asleep, no doubt dreaming of a remarkable marsupial and all our new friends.

It was after six when we arrived home. I thanked Gwen once again.

'Don't thank me, Pamela,' she said as we said our goodbyes. 'Nick was the one who wanted this day for you and Sharon. I suspect that he's busy with exams. You do realise that he loves you? I thought it when I saw you all on the ferry and he confirmed it on the phone when he suggested you two come instead of the three of you.'

'He shouldn't have told you that,' was my slightly angry comment.

'Pamela. He didn't tell me in words. He didn't need to. I hope you two work it out. You'd make a wonderful family, as I said when we first met.'

★ ★ ★

It was earlier than usual when I arrived at the centre on Wednesday. A quick yet thorough inspection revealed that all was in order, ready for the opening on Saturday morning. It had originally been intended to open on the Monday, but the centre manager wanted to maximise the Saturday morning crowd. Also we wished to check that people wouldn't end up queuing too long in peak times. The official opening remained Monday, but a dry run made sense, to iron out any bugs.

Brenda caught up with me when I'd been back to the office for only a few minutes. I wasn't prepared for her arriving so early and had been checking out some of our Skippy souvenirs.

'Hello, Pamela. How was your day out?'

I was minded to ignore her, though she was attempting to be courteous.

'Hello, Brenda. It was great. How was your meeting yesterday?'

Secretly I hoped Dave had fallen on his face.

'OK. I can see everything's almost finished.'

I filled her in with the latest info. 'Some scaffolding in the Santa workshop to repair lighting circuits. It'll be clear tomorrow. We can take a trial run in the afternoon if you wish. HJ and the centre manager too. Unfortunately Santa's helper won't be there until Saturday.'

Santa's helper was a lovely elderly guy who was perfect for the role. As I'd told Sharon, the Santas in stores and on the streets weren't the real Santa. However it was fine to tell the Santa helpers what you wanted for Christmas because they would let the real Santa know. I'd explained that he was busy preparing all the pressies for delivery on Christmas Eve.

Pressies? This country was turning my brains to mush. *Presents, Pamela*, I thought. *Stop speaking Australian. Next you'll end up with that strange nasal accent and calling women 'sheilas' and men 'blokes'.*

I shook myself. Brenda was at my desk, peering down at the photos I'd been examining.

'Dear Lord. It's you . . . and the actors from that telly show. You weren't lying about going there. How did you manage that?'

I was a little upset by her intrusion. I hadn't intended to share our special day out, especially with a person who'd dismissed my plans as the demented fantasy of some liar.

'I did tell you, Brenda. It was the woman who's life was saved by my Nick.' Although I could have disclosed the job offer from Gwen, it wasn't the appropriate time. Nor would it have done any good to reiterate that Dave stole my ideas.

Brenda was about to reply but must have decided that the atmosphere was too awkward.

'When Dave comes in, tell him to call me at Head Office. I'm going now. I'll see you tonight at the get-together?'

'Maybe. Maybe not. There isn't much point if I'm finishing work with you, is there?'

There was no reason to be polite any longer. I'd tried to play the game by the rules. The trouble was no one else did. Being employed by Gwen's firm? At least I could rely on her to believe me.

Dave walked in about fifteen minutes later. He stopped short, seeing me. I guessed yesterday hadn't gone well for him. Not that it mattered; my name was mud because of him.

I was past the point of niceties. So was he. No 'Hello Pamela,' or 'Nice day outside.' He marched up to my desk to stand over me.

I returned his scowl with an indifferent glance before returning to the paperwork I was doing. That seemed to infuriate him more, as I intended.

'You made me look like a right dag yesterday, you stupid sheila.' He was leaning over the desk, both hands resting on the Formica top.

I continued writing.

'You don't need my help for that, Mr Garrick.'

He smashed his closed fist against the

desk top. It hurt him, although he tried not to show it. Trying to remain composed, I put the pen down.

'You seem upset, Mr Garrick. Perhaps your conscience . . . ?'

'You think you're so smug and clever, don't you, Pamela? You in your short skirt and lipstick. You're a tart. No one takes you seriously, least of all your thicko mate, Brenda. She gave me a hard time yesterday in front of HJ. Wanted to know all the petty details of this bloody Train thing you dreamed up. Even asked me where I came up with the inspiration for it. Plus you didn't brief me the day before, like what I told you to.'

I remained seated, deliberately defusing his aggressive stance.

'I went on a Christmas submarine ride in Sydney last year. The kiddies loved the adventure. That's why I thought of the Train. Perhaps you might remember that detail next time you talk about 'your' brilliant Christmas idea, Dave.'

I'd had enough of this garbage. I stood up. With my heels on, I was as tall as him although a good fifty pounds lighter. I was beginning to worry that I'd pushed him too far. When would I learn to choose the time and place for my battles?

He shoved the desk to one side with both hands, breaking its leg as it was flung against a cabinet. I considered calling out before remembering how well insulated this office was. The same with the train tunnel. No one could hear me scream.

Desperately backing up, I stopped. The wall was at my back and the doorway was across the room. Dave took a step forward, raising an open hand. Tensing for his attack, I flung my arms up to cover my face, closing my eyes.

This was not going to end well.

11

Suddenly there was another sound; from outside this time. The door burst open.

'Quick, Kevin. Grab him,' some woman shouted. I heard footsteps pounding across the room then Dave struggling with someone as they crashed against furniture. My eyes opened. There was lots of banging as Kevin and Dave thrashed about, arms locked around each other. However my angry boss had no chance against the burly newcomer.

'Stop fighting me, Mr Garrick, or I'll have to hurt you bad. Nobody raises a hand to Pamela when I'm around.'

Understanding he was outmatched, Dave lowered his fists to his side. Kevin released him but stayed watching, ready to step in once more if required. I couldn't believe it.

Brenda entered, followed by Bruce, the snowman. There was real anger on their faces.

'What's the meaning of this, Brenda?' Dave demanded, composing himself. His torn shirt had been pulled out in the tussle with Kevin. He tucked it in in an attempt to restore his dignity.

Brenda ignored him, coming to my side.

'Are you OK, Pamela? We were outside. We had no idea he'd turn violent.'

'Me turn violent? You've got it all wrong, all of you. Pamela's a maniac. She tried to scratch my face. If you hadn't come in, I don't — ' He raised his arm but dropped it when Kevin pressed his own hands together and shifted his weight.

'Save your breath, Mr Garrick. You can't talk your way out of this one,' he said, clenching his own fists. His biceps were huge, accentuated by the blue work singlet he was wearing. He certainly wasn't in the mood for any more physical bluster on Dave's part.

'I'm OK — just a bit shaken. Thought I was in for it then.'

I moved further away from Dave. Brenda took my arm and guided me to a chair,.

'We were listening. Heard everything. I'm . . . There are no excuses. I believed what Dave told me. I had no idea how two-faced and devious he is. Had me and HJ totally convinced he'd dreamed this Train thing up by himself. Yesterday it became obvious that he didn't have a clue.'

Bruce stepped up. 'The wombat told Brenda and Mr Weatherly that he was good mates with me, then said I was called Bob. Reckon that's when Miss Brenda here sussed he was telling porkies. She came around this morning to get the truth about whose friend I was. Apparently this devious little nobody even tried to claim the snowstorm was his brainwave.'

I still was trying to piece it all together.

'Guess it was lucky you both came here when you did. Otherwise . . . ' I shuddered. Who would have thought Dave could lose his temper like that? The shattered desk was testament to what might have happened.

'Not luck. Kevin was fixing some cabling nearby and listening to me and Brenda. He mentioned that he'd seen Dave headed to yer office. Brenda guessed he might be upset so we dashed over here. Good thing we did, I reckon.'

'I reckon too, Bruce. Thank you all.' Then I had a thought. 'Brenda. You were leaving the building? That's what you told me.'

'Seeing those photos of yours got me thinking about how unjust I'd been, suspecting that you were the one making up stories. That's when I decided to catch up with Bruce.'

Dave was being very quiet, probably weighing up his options. He'd been well and truly exposed by his own shouted admission that he'd nicked my plan for

Christmas. I wondered what was going through his mind. Brenda addressed him.

'I think you'd best pack your private things and leave, Dave. Kevin will make certain that you find your way out. And don't expect any references . . . that is, unless you want any new employer to discover what the real Dave Garrick is like.'

Dave made a move towards Brenda and me but Kevin grabbed his shoulder.

'You can't sack me, Brenda. Only HJ can do that.' Dave looked smug. He knew he had a point.

'That's true,' admitted Brenda. 'HJ isn't available right now otherwise I'd phone him. Looks like you've got a reprieve for a day. Yet I can still have you removed from the premises.'

'On what grounds, lady?'

'Safety considerations. You threatened a fellow staff member. Perhaps we should involve the police. What do you think, Kevin?'

'Just leave us alone for five minutes, Brenda. No need for police then. Maybe the ambos.'

I saw Dave go pale.

'No need for that. However I'm making a promise, Brenda. I'm not finished with you . . . or the tart.' He stared at me with such hatred, I felt myself shiver. Resigned to leaving, he went to his desk and pushed things into an empty box.

'Oh. Don't forget your signed photos, Dave,' I said as bravely as I could. The guy had really scared me, though I was trying not to show it. He grudgingly picked them out of the filing cabinet.

Brenda decided to speak up too.

'One other thing from me, Dave. Pamela's 'thicko mate' is going to tell everyone here what you tried to do. If you show your ugly face around here again, it'll be open season.'

It was clear that Brenda had heard the names he'd called us both. 'Open season' was a not-so-veiled threat that Kevin would pass on to his fellow builders and contractors. We had a close knit team that stood together if anyone did the wrong thing, especially to us women.

Kevin gave him a gentle shove. I hoped it was the last I'd see of Dave Garrick. At that moment I remembered his chilling vindictive comment. *I'm not finished with you . . . or the tart.* Was it bluster or was Dave Garrick the type of bloke who kept his promises?

★ ★ ★

Once Kevin, Dave and Bruce had departed, I bent down to pick up the scattered items from my desk. My treasured framed photo of Sharon was on the floor, the glass cracked. That could be easily replaced. However the memory of Dave raising his hand caused me to pause.

'Sit yourself down, Pamela. You've had a nasty shock. I had no idea what an evil bastard he is.' Brenda busied herself making some tea for us both.

'It's not that, Brenda,' I explained. 'I've dealt with women haters before. It's just . . . today, I felt so helpless. Normally I can stand up for myself, as you know.'

'Got that right, Pamela. It's one thing I've always admired about you. All the guys on site think the world of you and they respect you for being so strong.'

She passed me a cup. When I took a sip I almost choked.

'Sugar. It's good for shock,' she said.

'I'm surprised you managed to fit any water in. How many spoonfuls?'

'Only two.' I looked at her quizzically. 'Of course, they were soup spoons,' she admitted with a grin.

'What happens now? I mean, with my job?'

'I'll try to get an extension on your contract but it's not up to me. I'm positive HJ will back me about giving Dastardly Dave the boot, especially after today's performance. I just cannot understand how he convinced us he was the wronged party. He'd make one helluva politician.'

Brenda was trying to distract me from my self-doubts. All of this time I thought I didn't want a man to support me; that all I needed was Sharon to make my life complete.

Momentarily I thought of Nick. Who was this other woman in his life? If it was as innocent as he'd said, all he had to do was explain. Was it too much to ask?

One of the female assistants came a bit later to help me finish tidying up. My desk was beyond repair so I decided to commander Dave's. It took a little while to disinfect it to my satisfaction.

★   ★   ★

The remainder of the day was quite tranquil. I spent most of it doing last-minute checks. The train started up without problems, though we only ran it a short distance. That scaffolding over the line further in was still being used by the electricians.

Walking through the illuminated tunnel with Bruce, I confessed I doubted I could actually travel on the Train myself — even with Sharon.

'The tunnel doesn't look spooky with the safety lamps on, Bruce, but switch them off and I'd be scared as anything.'

He seemed to understand about my phobia, probably more so than other men.

'Yer not alone, Pamela. I don't normally confess this to anyone but I believe yer won't laugh like me mates did at school . . . *Clowns*. That's what scares me. Can you credit that? Bloody smiling clowns. Even just thinking about their painted faces . . . ' He shuddered.

'Good thing there aren't any clowns hiding in here then, Bruce,' I reassured him, making a mental note to substitute one of the toys in Santa's workshop. I'd heard about this phobia and didn't want to traumatise any children who might share Bruce's aversion.

'OK. Imagine we're on Santa's Train in the dark tunnel waiting to arrive at the North Pole. Talk me through it.'

'The air con's going all the time. Chilly but not too cold. I've decided on forty-five degrees. After all, no one will be wearing cardies or pullovers, will they? As the train passes this point it triggers the Snow Maker so, by the time they come out of the tunnel it's snowing all around the train. It stops again as they re-enter the tunnel heading for the reindeer. As it melts the water's used again for more snow. It's called recycling. More efficient.'

'Is there a manual switch? I want to witness this for myself.'

'Thought yer might, Pamela. See that little red toggle switch on the wall?'

I flipped it and we made our way to the first scene; the village we now called Christmastown. Exiting the tunnel, Bruce flipped another switch and the safety lamps went off, leaving soft blue ambient lighting to illuminate the village. Tiny street lamps and twinkling Christmas tree lights completed the spectacle.

All around us, snow was fluttering through the air. I held out my hand to examine the flake that landed on it. It melted before my eyes.

'Well?' Bruce asked.

'Magical. Beautifully magical, Bruce. You've made my dream come true.' I wiped a tear from my eye as we stood side by side, lovely white snow flakes dancing in the air. A snowstorm in Sydney around Christmas? This would be the perfect Yuletide treat for everyone.

★   ★   ★

At five-thirty the centre closed. That meant our party in the extension would be a private affair. One thing I'd noticed that was markedly different between here and home was that the pubs filled up with blokes after work, then gradually emptied out as the men staggered home to the missus, a meat pie and mash.

In Manchester, at least, men tended to go straight home for supper then go to the hotel before closing time for a swift half and maybe a game of dominoes or darts.

The men and women on site had done a great job. Most had only spent a few days, seconded to help out with the Train but some had been with me almost every day, making certain that everything was done ready for the run-up to Christmas starting Saturday.

I never begrudged anyone drinking alcohol and I didn't mind the occasional drink myself. It didn't take long before the bottles of beer and spirits were being opened along with a tinnie or two. HJ was a decent employer, his motto being 'Work hard, play hard.' There was a wide choice of drinks supplied by HJ, including some soft drinks for those few who preferred to not get drunk or who were driving home.

'Can I pour you that disgusting pineapple juice, Pamela?' Kev asked me. 'Everyone realises you love it, but it's so sickly. Give me a Fosters any time.'

Brenda had put a large bottle of my preferred beverage on the table. There was a note saying *Pamela Only* fixed on the side with sticky tape.

Taking a mouthful from a paper cup, I was inclined to agree with Kevin. It tasted funny; a different brand to my favourite.

It was comforting to be here with my friends. I'd noticed Kev was keeping an eye out for me, probably following Brenda's suggestion. His wife was one of my set painters. She was here too. They made a lovely couple and, judging by her comments to me, it wouldn't be too long until she'd be on maternity leave.

Brenda came over later, pulling me to one side.

'I thought you should be told right away. HJ rang me back and left a message. He's dismissed Dave and apologises profusely for what has happened. He'll see you in person when we have the trial run tomorrow night. You'll be going to the carol singing in the old centre tomorrow night too, won't you? Seeing Nick again?'

'Yes to both questions. He and I, we really need to sort out things between us.'

She turned to leave but reconsidered.

'Don't want you getting upset, but Dave turned up here an hour ago. Reckoned he was still entitled to come to this get-together. Two of the plasterers put him right. They weren't too polite about it, either.'

Despite her reassurances, I felt a little shocked at his brazen attitude turning up again. It seemed that Dave was the sort of bloke who blamed everyone else for his misfortunes.

I went down to the temporary site office to phone for a taxi. The newly enclosed extension to Waratah World was closed off from the original centre by time locks to make certain that no one could get into the working shop area after six o'clock. That meant a lengthy walk through the ghost town of the still incomplete interior down to the exit at the far end.

I arranged for the taxi to pick me up in twenty minutes. That left enough time to say goodbyes and grab my bag from the little office near the Train exhibit. I headed for there and was about to pass the entrance area for Santa's Train when I heard footsteps from behind me. It was then that I had a dizzy turn, realising I'd been weaving from side to side for the past dozen steps.

All of a sudden my legs went from under me causing me to stumble against some unpainted concrete column. It knocked the wind out of me.

It was a good thing no one saw me, I decided. Probably think I was drunk or something. I tried to stand up straight but faintness caused my head to swirl as my left leg collapsed again, breaking the heel of my shoe as I struggled to balance.

There was enough light pouring through the overhead domes fifty feet above me, yet the surroundings were blurry. I propped myself against the column then reached down to take off my shoes, one by one. My panty hose were torn too. There was a pair of flat shoes in my office. I was going there anyway for ... for ... I couldn't remember.

'Hello, Pamela. Looks like you need a hand.'

I spun around at the vaguely familiar voice. It made me feel fainter. Dropping my shoes, I tried to focus on the voice as the figure of a man appeared from the darkened Train ticketing hall.

'Is sat you, Dave? Yous ... yous shouldn't be ... '

Why did my words come out wrong?

'Yeah. It's me, Pamela. Are you enjoying my little pressie in your fruit juice?'

Pressie? Present? 'Yous push shome-
thing in my drink.'

'Vodka. Don't you recall telling me
why you don't drink spirits? Makes you
all sleepy, you said. Figured it would
make you . . . shall we say . . . less feisty
for what I have in mind. Not that I
fancy loud-mouthed sheilas but I know
you want it, short skirts and all. I
thought we'd take a little trip before-
hand. Just you and me and that bloody
train of yours.'

I couldn't concentrate. A trip?
Where? Dave had grabbed my arm.

'Help . . . Help me, shomebody.' I
screamed as loudly as I could.

Dave didn't react. That was the
scariest part.

'No one around to hear, you
dim-witted broad. And in that bloody
tunnel of yours, there's even less
chance. Remember all that sound
insulation you had installed? Perfect for
what I have in mind.'

He dragged me out of the light-filled
main passageway with its mezzanine

256

level of still empty shops. The brightly coloured signs and large room where train passengers would be queuing excitedly in a few days, was now unlit and foreboding. There were no windows, only the ticket booth and roped off lines leading to the 'station'.

Black holes of tunnels were on either side of the engine and carriages — one where a crowded train would enter the adventure world of Santa's North Pole and the other where the empty train would reappear to collect the next group of travellers.

I stared at the Stygian black abyss that Dave was pushing me towards. He meant to assault me in there. Vainly I struggled to break his grip. He laughed. I simply couldn't think properly amid the fear of that blackness.

'Do you honestly think I'm going to drag you into the dark, Pamela? No. You can relax.' He laughed. I smelled stale beer on his breath. 'I want to see what I'm getting. Right. Where's the master switch?'

Pulling me to the ticket booth, he reached inside to press some buttons. The ticketing area burst into light, flashing lamps illuminating the booth and *Santa's Train* sign.

'On second thoughts ... ' He pressed two switches and the area returned to its former dimness, leaving the train and safety lighting visible in the twin dark semi-circles of the tunnel. 'Can't have any nosy security guard interrupting our private party, can we, girlie?'

I stared at his face in the half-light. His eyes were wide, and he was dribbling slightly. He was totally mad.

'Pleash, Dave. You don't wanna do this,' I pleaded.

'Oh yes, I do, Pamela. You've screwed up my life big time. And if you're thinking they'll catch me for what I'm going to do, forget it. I'm clearing off straight after.'

He flung one arm wide like a circus ringmaster. 'Showtime, Pamela. Guess who's going to be the main attraction?'

I lashed out with my hands and feet. It did no good. He was too strong for me in my drunken state. Then he dragged me onto the engine before pushing me roughly onto the seat.

'All aboard,' he chuckled, donning the elf hat that the driver would be wearing. The train was electric and moved off quietly as he engaged the throttle.

It was fortunate that the safety lighting shone throughout the winding journey. It gave me a chance to think, to try and fight the debilitating effects that the alcohol he'd somehow spiked my drink with. The adrenalin that had shot through my system at seeing the darkness, seemed to help focus my mind.

Driving on the track . . . there was a warning in my mind. The scaffolding. It was at the fifth opening, straddling the track.

We'd already passed the first two vistas. I had to stop this maniac before he killed us both.

'Shop the train, you idiot. The track'sh blocked,' I shouted frantically.

'Nice try, lady. Perhaps I should speed her up. Reckon that bed in Mrs Santa's home should be just big enough for us.'

'Sthop the train. Now.'

He wasn't listening. It was up to me. The emergency power switch was on the driver's console and, through the fuzziness that was my brain, I recalled reading that it would disable the motor for at least ten minutes. The trouble was, Mad Dave was between me and it.

I had to distract him somehow. What with? My shoes were back in the main part of the extension and there was nothing else around. At that point I brushed my hand through my hair in frustration. There were only seconds left. We'd passed the third vista.

A bobby pin. Would that work? I pulled it out from my hair and bent it straight while Dave faced forward then jabbed him in the back of his knee, struggling forward past him to press the red Stop button.

Dave swung his arm, smashing my body against the cab side. I heard my shoulder crack as the train began to slow. Would it stop in time? We rounded the corner and emerged from the tunnel. Dozens of scaffolding pipes, like a kids' construction set, stood there. I prayed we'd stop in time as the engine rolled inch by inch towards them. Then they began to tumble, one by one.

Dave swore. There was a cacophony of crashing metal on metal, deafening me, as the intricate framework collapsed like a deck of cards all around. Dave jumped out as I fought to stand.

Metal pipes smashed onto the top of the cab, the engine teetering under the weight until it began to tip, still moving forward through more and more pipes. Cables joined in the iron deluge, torn from the ceiling conduits. I had to get out too but my shoulder screamed in pain with every movement. Dislocated? Broken?

'Dave. Help me!' I shouted. He

turned momentarily then resumed his escape, leaving me for dead. The bastard!

A metal bar on the ground caused him to trip before a huge ten-foot plank slid from its now precarious perch up above to crash down on top of him.

'Dave!'

He didn't move. In the dim light from above, a pool of blackness seeped across the concrete floor under his body.

It was up to me. I launched myself through the open panelling of the engine just as it finally tipped to the right, the left wheels no longer on the track. The carpet of Santa's house helped cushion my fall yet the momentum threw me against a sturdy desk. For a second time today, the breath was knocked from my lungs.

My shoulder hurt so much. It was a struggle to open my eyes. Feeling my forehead with my free hand, it was wet. My fingers were dark red.

The thunderous noise had stopped.

Everywhere was a chaotic scene of destruction, pipes covering toys and splintered furniture. Mrs Claus was lying on her side, pen still clutched in her pink plastic hand. The train engine rested at an impossible angle, most wheels teetering above of the track.

I tried to move my feet but couldn't. Looking down from my twisted sitting position, I could see a huge plank compressing them.

'Dave. For God's sake. Help me.' My cries were rasping and softer as dust filled the air.

There was only an eerie silence. Slowly I forced my head to turn. Dave lay under pipes and rubble, unmoving.

No one could hear us. They had probably gone home. If the crash hadn't been heard, then my feeble voice wouldn't be either.

There was nothing I could do to help either of us. At least the lights were still on. The prospect of being here in the dark as well would have been too much for me.

There was a sound from one side. Was a rescuer coming?

'Over here! I'm injured. Dave too.'

No one answered. I began to call again, stopping when I heard the sound again. This time it lasted longer. Where? There was movement to one side, my peripheral vision saw it.

'Here!' I called out, wiping blood from my eyes. A section of scaffold shifted. It was balanced precariously near the main power cables that dangled from the ceiling like twisted spaghetti.

'NOOOO!'

Another small sound was followed by metal contorting and shifting slowly. Then there was the shrill racket of another collapse reverberating through the structure. The lights flickered once . . . twice . . . as the cables strained to stay intact. Finally, the sparking electrical wiring ripped apart.

I screamed.

The tomb-like cavern of Santa's Train had been plunged into pure, terrifying and absolute night.

12

I don't know how long I lay there. If I could have curled myself into a ball or foetal shape to protect myself, I would have. But my legs were pinned, and as for my shoulder . . .

The slightest movement sent waves of agony through my body. So I sat there, unmoving, my entire body shrieking inside for release from this hell hole of blackness. From time to time there was a creak or metallic scrape as debris shifted or slipped further.

There was nothing I could do.

My eyes were open as much as I could manage, searching for a glimmer or twinkle of light; anything to give me hope and save me from the suffocating ink-black shroud that was smothering me.

Then I noticed my breathing was

shallow and rapid. Hyperventilation. I was having a panic attack only this time there was no one to calm me down; no Mum with her soothing voice, no Dad telling me The Dark can't hurt me.

I concentrated, as I'd been taught as a child.

'Breathe slower, Pamela. Slower. That's my girl,' I heard Dad saying to me, his deep voice sounding so hypnotic and reassuring.

I listened intently. There was another noise apart from my heartbeat and breathing. Faint. Human. Afraid. Someone else was trapped.

'Dave,' I tried to call. My throat ached from the dust. Only echoes replied.

Not Dave. It was a child, whimpering . . . mewling. She was coming closer.

'Hello?'

More quiet crying before a hesitant voice.

'Hel . . . hello?'

'What's your name?' I didn't want to alarm her any more.

'Pa . . . Pa . . . Pammy. I'm so . . . so
. . . scared.'

I couldn't see her, though she was
closer.

'It's all right, Pammy. I'm here.'

I sensed her close by, her little hand
touching me tentatively as she moved to
snuggle by my side.

'The m . . . m . . . monsters are
coming.'

'You're safe, Pammy. There are no
monsters.' *Apart from men like my
boss*, I realised. My drunken state was
wearing off. Now I had other horrors to
contend with.

She was trembling, her skin cold
from shock. Her fingers felt so thin, not
like my Sharon's.

*Oh Lord. Sharon. What if I die here?
What will happen to my darling
daughter?*

You're not going to die, Pamela, my
logical self decided. *Your injuries aren't
life-threatening.*

Dave's, on the other hand, were. It
was up to me to go for help.

Easier said than done. Without The Dark, I might have had a chance. I couldn't go forward to Santa's Grotto, even though that would have been a far shorter route. The passageway and tunnel were blocked. I'd seen that much before the lights went out.

I felt the girl nudge a corner of my mind again. She wasn't real; a part of me understood that. Equally well, some of my thoughts were struggling to cope with the trauma of my phobia and injuries, searching for a way to control the dread that threatend to overwhelm me.

'My name's Pamela too.' She nestled closer then jumped as tendrils of wiring touched our faces and arms. I could smell a horrible odour. So could she. She tried to cover her nose.

'What is it, Pamela?'

I fought to keep my stomach from retching.

'It's nothing, Pammy. Mothballs. A chemical called naphthalene. It keeps moths away from clothes because they don't like the smell.'

There was a pause. 'Nappylene? That's a funny word.' She sniffed the air.

'It's not that bad, Pamela. It's to scare moths . . . not people. Go on. You sniff it.'

I did; very gingerly at first. The memory of those mothballs wasn't so repulsive now. Taking a deeper breath, I wondered why the odour should be so repugnant. Usually they're only put in clothes in a cupboard or wardrobe.

The blood on my forehead was still wet. The feeling in both legs was getting less. I wondered if the circulation had been restricted.

'We have to leave here, Pammy.'

'We can't. The door's locked. Granny has the key. It's too hard.'

My brain was in turmoil. What was too hard? The door? No . . . lifting the scaffolding wood.

'I can't see, Pamela. I'm getting frightened again.'

She was right. The Dark closed in on

us once more. My heart began to race again.

'Don't let it win, Pammy. It's not going to hurt you.'

The sounds of her whimpering began anew as we each closed our eyes tight to hide from it, each fighting against another panic attack.

'Listen, Pammy. Listen to me. The Dark can't hurt us when our eyes are closed. We do it all the time when we're asleep. We're not afraid then, are we?'

Her heart rate slowed a little. 'I su — suppose.'

'Keep your eyes closed, like me. Pretend you're going to sleep. Don't open your eyes at all.'

Our breathing slowed.

'It's working, Pamela. When . . . when our eyes are closed, The Dark can't see us. She can't hurt us.'

She? Pammy called the Dark 'she'. My God. Where was Pammy? What had Granny Balitsky done to us? More crucially, how could I have forgotten this childhood trauma?

'Pammy. I need your help. No, don't open your eyes at all. We must move the wood on my legs. Try to lift it with me.' We reached forward, grasping the edge of the plank by touch alone. It wouldn't budge.

'Leverage. We need a lever.'

'One of these metal bars, Pamela?'

'Yes, move it under the wood. Careful. Not near our legs. Now push it down. Hard. As hard as you can.'

The wood shifted upwards until I felt the pressure lighten on my shins. Then it dropped. The pain surged through my entire body, slowly abating as I fought to stay conscious. My bitten lips were bleeding now. The taste was almost metallic.

'Try again, Pammy. We must try again.'

This time the plank slipped away to one side.

I moved my legs, careful not to drop the plank back onto them. Reaching down with my free hand, I had to grit my teeth from the shoulder pain. There was no break, though I could feel sticky blood on my panty hose.

'Can we look now, Pamela?'

'No, little one. Come with me. I'll take you away from here.'

Easier said than done. There was no possibility of putting any weight on my feet. That meant dragging myself back the way we came, probably with a dislocated shoulder. There was no other way.

Follow the rails, past Dave. In spite of what he'd done, I had to save him.

Fortunately there was no gravel on these minature train tracks. They were firmly bolted to the floor. I grabbed one rail and pulled myself along, grimacing from the agony. Repeat the move; reach out, grip and pull.

'Why were you in The Dark?' I asked my imaginary younger self in an attempt to diminish the tedious ache.

'I'm bad. Granny punishes me. Every day she locks me under the stairs. The monsters wait there for me to come. She tells me they're there, waiting to attack me unless I'm very still and quiet. They eat naughty girls. I don't want them to eat me.'

I remembered now. How could she? Doing that to her own granddaughter, who was in her care? I burst into tears, stopping my exertions.

'The monster,' I sobbed, opening my eyes for an instant.

'No. The monsters. They'll find us, Pamela. Close your eyes again. Please. Quickly. Before they see us.'

I gritted my teeth, wiped my eyes and reached forward once again. This time I forced myself to keep looking. I wasn't going to fear any bloody darkness ever again.

'Pamela! The monsters!'

'The only monster is Granny, Pammy. Can't you understand that? *She* hurt you. She hurt *us* with her horror stories about The Dark, and locking you in that horrible cupboard for hours on end.'

One more foot forward. *Push the pain aside. Think of Granny. Hate her and what she's done. Use that hatred.*

'Can I open my eyes too?' Her voice was pleading, asking me for permission to face her fears at last.

'Yes. There's nothing here, Pammy. Nothing to be terrified of any longer.'

Her relief surged through me, redoubling my strength to press onwards. At last, there was a lightening; black turning to shades of grey. We emerged into the ticketing area and, although there were no lights there, the main concourse lighting seeped through the closed doors. A shadow passed by, blocking the bright slits momentarily.

'Help,' I shouted weakly from the tracks, praying that I wouldn't have to struggle any further. My voice was no more than a raspy whisper. I breathed deeply, almost fainting from the shoulder pain.

'HELP!'

Footsteps sounded as the twin doors were flung open. All I could see were three silhouettes rushing towards me.

'Pamela! What happened?' Brenda

cried, kneeling down. The lights were switched on. I heard them all gasp. Not one of my prettiest moments, I guessed. She called to Kevin to phone for an ambulance.

'Tunnel collapse. Dave's injured.'

'I'll get the fire brigade, too.'

Brenda tried to move me but it was too much for my injured body. I closed my eyes and let myself succumb to the bliss of oblivion. We'd beaten The Dark — Pammy and me.

13

The following hours and days were a muddled blur. I recall waking in the ambulance, its siren blaring away. Every part of me hurt. Brenda was there by my side, crying a lot. I tried to speak but all that came out was a load of gibberish.

The next time was in hospital. It was night-time and smelled of disinfectant and antiseptic.

'We're going to reset your shoulder, Mrs Grant. It might hurt a bit.'

It hurt more than a bit. I must have passed out again. If I ever found out the name of that doctor, I'd make certain he never had a Chrissie card from me.

Morning came. I was in a bed. It looked like a private room.

A familiar face leaned over mine.

'She's awake, nurse.' Nick was there,

holding my bandaged hand. He hadn't shaved.

'She's the cat's mother,' I managed to say.

'Is Mrs Grant usually this lippy?' the blue-clad nurse asked as she checked my pulse with her pendant necklace watch.

'As a matter of fact, she is. Wouldn't want her any other way.'

'What are you doing here?' I said. I tried to turn my head to see the time on a wall clock. It wasn't a good idea.

'Wanted to check on you before going to school. Sharon — '

'Hell. Sharon?' I began to panic. I'd forgotten.

'Sharon's fine. She stayed with Mrs de Luca last night. I wanted to check an idea with you this morning though. Mum and Dad have offered to help look after her until you're back on those sexy legs of yours. Mrs de Luca's great but she needs some help.'

I was surprised. 'Your parents?' Did I trust them with my precious daughter?

After all, our first meeting hadn't been great.

There was no other option I could think of, though. Mrs D was fine for a few hours, but to expect her to care for Sharon full-time?

'Yes please.' I was so exhausted. Nick squeezed my hand then bent to kiss my forehead.

'Have to leave now. I'll be back later this arvo. Love you.'

'Love you too,' I replied without thinking. Closing my eyes for a moment, I opened them to say something more, but he was gone.

The nurse adjusted my bedding.

'Your boyfriend's been here since midnight. He was very concerned.'

'No, he's not my . . . ' I tried to say before dozing off again.

★ ★ ★

It was Friday morning before I was able to sit up. Nick had returned as promised with a bag full of toiletries and underwear that Mrs D had packed for me.

Evidently he'd managed to shave and change before returning. He assured me Sharon was fine and was staying the night at his place with his parents. She'd been very concerned about me, enough to make a beautiful card and painting to cheer me up.

When Brenda arrived, I had a hundred and one questions for her. Nick sat in a corner, marking some papers, while I tried to find out everything that had happened since Wednesday night.

'I can't afford a private room, Brenda. Why insist on one?'

The nurse had told me about my admission.

'The company are paying for everything, Pamela. Least we could do. As long as you're here, you're getting nothing but the best.'

I breathed a sigh of relief and thanked her. It had been a worry.

I explained as well as I could what

had occurred on Wednesday night. It was hazy.

'What about Dave? Is he . . . ?'

'Still alive? Unfortunately. What he did to you, Pamela — plus what he tried to do . . . I cannot believe we worked with that . . . bastard. He has a broken arm and concussion. They've patched him up and discharged him this morning.'

I couldn't believe it.

'They let him go?'

'The police took him away. He's in jail; I'm guessing for a long time, kidnapping, assault, criminal damage and a dozen or two other charges. HJ insisted on it. He's friends with the Commissioner.'

It took a few moments for me to digest all those details. Initially I felt a touch of sorrow for him before remembering that train ride to hell.

'Dave put alcohol in my fruit juice.'

'We worked it out. After you left to ring for the taxi, Kevin's wife thought she'd try some of your bottle. She noticed the vodka straight away.'

'I should have, I suppose. My sense of taste isn't great. Plus I've never touched vodka.'

'Anyway,' continued Brenda, 'we surmised that you might be drunk without realising it. We spent ages searching and found your shoes. Looked in the Train area too but clearly never thought what Dave had chosen to do. When you crawled out of there, raving on about monsters . . . Well you're on the mend now. That's what counts.'

'And the Train? Was there much damage?'

Tomorrow's grand opening seemed highly unlikely to happen now.

'Your team were brilliant. They worked through yesterday, last night and today. I've just come from there. The test run was perfect. Amazing what a bit of sticky tape can do.'

She was joking about the tape, though I was hugely relieved that Santa's Train was literally back on track.

'As for you, young lady, you're on paid sick leave for as long as you need. A few more days in here to make certain you're ... oh, what's that expression they use in those British films?'

Nick chirped up from his corner.

'Tickety-boo, Brenda.'

I winced, not from the physical pain.

Once Brenda had left, I was alone with Nick. The fact that I was lying on a bed in some sort of itchy cloth garment didn't escape me ... or Nick.

'Seeing you like this, Pamela, is like a dream.'

I laughed. There were bandages on the cuts to my arms and legs, my ankles were swollen but thankfully under a sheet, and there was a linen dressing on my forehead. In addition, I had my glasses on. I hated them, but wearing contacts in here wasn't practical at all.

'You must have some very way-out dreams, Mr Winters.'

'No. Not that. Simply being alone with you without distractions. I do realise my exaggerated age wasn't fair to you. I didn't want you to believe I was some young bloke who couldn't be taken seriously.'

'Even though that's exactly what you are, Nick. Young. No life experience to speak of. You're not thinking straight. Men should go out with younger women, not somebody six years older. It's an unspoken law.'

'Unspoken, yes. Law, no. Conventions are being broken all the time. I heard they're training women astronauts, there are ladies in Parliament and men like your ex-boss are a part of a dying generation. What about you and those mini-skirts you wear? Is that conventional? Working in a man's job?'

'It's hardly the same thing as having a relationship . . . getting married. I'll be honest, Nick, young feller me lad. I do fancy you, a lot. More than you realise. In that tunnel, it was your face that helped keep me going . . . yours and Sharon's. You do realise I'm stuck in Sydney for the foreseeable future?'

He nodded. His green eyes appeared even more intense as I stared at him.

'Oh yes, and Pamela — I just thought of an item I noticed while you were snoring your head off the other night. It was on your medical chart. Any guesses?'

I shifted uncomfortably, suddenly deciding to examine my nail varnish in detail.

'Let me give you a clue, Disingenuous Lass. I'm twenty-three, not twenty-six, and you told me you were twenty-nine. Isn't that true?'

Damn. He knew. So much for any future possibilities. No point bluffing it out.

'I . . . I may have been a smidgen on the economical side. After all, I'd met you only a few minutes earlier at Brenda's place. How could I predict the future?'

His silence made me feel guiltier. I'd been so angry at him telling porkies about his age.

'Damn it, Nick. All right. You've seen

my date of birth, I assume. I lied. I'm thirty. Three-zero. Thirty. Happy now?'

'I still love you, Pamela. And you said you loved me yesterday.'

'Did I? Must have been delirious from the drugs and Dave's blinking alcohol.' I decided to adopt a more serious tone. 'We still have that problem between us. Your other woman. If it's innocent — though I can't imagine how — why not tell me the truth about your relationship? To me, it seems she's your second choice if I break up with you.'

'Again.'

'All right, Nick. Again. You're the one who keeps coming back to me, despite my actions.'

Nick considered the situation.

'If I could tell you, Pamela, I would. I made a promise to her. She's very vulnerable, not strong like you. I'll ask her again if I can disclose the truth to you and hopefully you'll understand. I don't want to lose you. The other night — '

I noticed tears in his eyes and his

voice becoming unsteady.

'What about the other night? None of my injuries were life-threatening . . . '

His silence prompted me to sit up. It hurt in a different place. I noticed bruising on my stomach as I peeked under the sheet.

'Some clot in your leg. They gave you a drug called heparin in your tummy to dissolve it. If it had moved . . . '

Nick didn't finish his revelation. It was a sobering thought. No wonder he'd been so attentive and concerned.

I tried to dismiss his shocking news as well as I could, turning the subject away from what might have been. Dave deserved some serious jail time for all that he'd done to me. The thought of Sharon being without her mother as well as her father was dreadful.

'Tell you what, Mr Nick Winters. If you can explain away this other lady in your life to my satisfaction, I might consider giving you a kiss and we could take it from there.'

'Let's see — engagement, marriage,

three brothers and sisters for Sharon as well as a house? Oh yeah, and a Victa lawnmower of our very own?'

I burst into a fit of laughter, instantly regretting it thanks to the renewed pain. When it subsided, I had to explain that a kiss simply meant a kiss.

'As for the rest? We'll have to wait and see.'

★   ★   ★

Saturday was the day the Train would begin running. I wished I were there to see it, as well as the joy on faces both young and old. Instead I was stuck in here until at least Monday.

On the plus side, I would be able to go to a proper toilet and have a shower. Despite the bed baths, I decided I was getting too whiffy.

Besides, Sharon was coming in to visit with Nick. I'd missed her so much, showing her photo to all the nurses until I was sure they were afraid to come into the room any more.

Being in a private room had its advantages but the times I was by myself seemed interminable. Nick had offered to bring in his collection of X-Men comics but I politely declined.

I lay back counting the plaster flowers on the ceiling yet again before deciding that there might be some article or advertisement in the Australian Woman's Weekly that I hadn't yet memorised by heart.

Nick was coming in the afternoon with Sharon and his mum. Sharon had apparently stayed there Thursday and Friday nights. That left me a few hours of nothing to do as well as no one to do it with. At least I could now appreciate where the expression 'dying of boredom' came from.

There was a knock on the door. I called out 'Come on in,' expecting a nurse with a cup of tea. Hospital tea tasted more like dishwater; however it was hot, plus the bikkies dulled the insipid taste.

I wasn't prepared for this visitor,

though. It was Nick's other woman.

I scrunched myself up so that I was sitting, the emergency buzzer within easy reach.

'Hello. You must be Pamela.' She brushed her long blonde hair from her forehead before firmly closing the door and approaching my bed. Her manner seemed apprehensive and the tone of her voice a little scared.

'Nick told me you were wanting to find out about me, so here I am. Before we start, I have to tell you that I love him too and no one — absolutely no one — is going to take him away from me.'

14

I looked steadily at my visitor. 'Suppose you tell me who you are, miss.' She wasn't wearing a wedding ring. 'It's only polite to disclose who's having a go at me. As you might have gathered, I've not had one of my better weeks.'

My tone was quite confrontational — though I was far from fit to face another homicidal maniac.

She took a step back.

'I'm sorry, Pamela. I didn't mean to alarm you. It's just . . . coming here . . . speaking to you. It's difficult for me. May I?'

She pulled a chair towards the bed, then sat down. Her body language told me she was far from comfortable at being here.

'I'm Carol.' She held out her hand. I took it and we shook hands, though her grip was loose and her palms cold to the touch.

Carol. Was that supposed to mean something? Oh . . . A light dawned.

'You're Nick's younger sister. The one I was told not to mention to your mum and dad? Sorry, Carol. The way Nick warned me not to say your name — I honestly thought you were dead.'

It was the wrong thing to say. Her eyes were sunken and dark, her body thin, almost emaciated. She was not a well woman. I should have seen that earlier; however all I could perceive until now was a rival.

'I'd better go. Coming here to see you was a mistake. If Nick hadn't pleaded with me . . . '

I reached out to her.

'No. Stay. It's . . . I need to understand. I promise I won't hurt you. You have a son?'

That question appeared to engage Carol. I sensed a relaxation in her apprehension as she ceased trying to pull away.

'Liam. Nick's taking care of him while I'm here. Nick's been really good to us.'

Reaching over to my bedside table, I took a clean cup and poured her some cordial. Carol took the cup in both hands. They were shaking as she gulped the liquid down noisily.

'I'm afraid I don't understand, Carol. Why do you want Nick visiting you to be a secret?'

She took a deep breath, glancing around the room as though making certain we were alone. I realised how petrified I'd been in the darkness and that she appeared to be the same. In her case it was seemingly a state of mind with her. Sadly, not all women had my resilience or belief in themselves.

'I did a stupid thing, Pamela. I became pregnant.' I was about to say that being with child wasn't stupid when she qualified it. 'I wasn't married. What's worse, the man I thought I loved left me. I found out later from a

friend that he was already married. I'd
only just left school, planning to go to
university.'

I could now guess where this was
heading. Unmarried mother — her
parents not wanting her name mentioned in the house. Thinking back to
my visit to the Winters' home, there
were no photos of Carol on display
— otherwise I might have deduced who
Nick's mystery woman was well before
now.

'How long since you saw your
parents, Carol?'

'Not since I told them. They blamed
me — even Mum. Nothing said about
the bloke who seduced me. Nothing at
all. It was as though the whole situation
was my fault alone. It's not fair.'

It wasn't fair — but unfortunately it
was still the way some attitudes were.

We continued to speak, with her
opening up more and more to me,
woman to woman.

'I went interstate for a few years
. . . had Liam there. It's very difficult to

work and care for a toddler — accommodation, food — you can understand. So I drifted back here. I kept in contact with Nick. He's been fantastic with money to help us out, and finding me a babysitter and a part time job.'

'But you're not well, Carol. It's noticeable. Perhaps if your mum and dad knew?'

She stood up. A wave of panic crossed her once-pretty features.

'No . . . no . . . They can't find out. They might stop Nick being there for me. Dad especially. He was livid about me becoming pregnant. I've written to them a few times. They've never written back.'

'They've never seen Liam?'

'Never.'

At that moment I decided I had a family to mend if I could. Also I was able to allow my heart to take control of my relationship with Nick. I'd been wrong to doubt him, wrong to judge him and right now all I wanted was to apologise.

Maybe it was fate that stopped me taking Sharon back to England. Maybe not. However if we were to stay here, I wanted Nick to be a part of our future.

Before Carol left, I gave her a hug. Whatever happened between her and her parents, I was determined to befriend her.

★ ★ ★

Nick arrived with Sharon that afternoon. The normal rules for visiting times didn't appear to apply to lucky patients in private rooms.

Seeing Sharon for the first time since the accident was emotional for us both. Sharon had never been to a 'hostipal' before. Her initial shyness was soon gone as I explained simply and clearly why I was here.

She was eager to share her own adventures. Nancy and Arthur had taken her to her favourite playground, as well as a more local one where they'd flown a kite. Arthur was also willing to play Snakes and Ladders and Ker-Plunk a lot.

Then it was Nick's turn. They'd obviously talked in the car on the drive over.

'Do you remember when I asked you if you'd mind when Mummy and I kissed?' he said.

'Yes, I 'member. I told you it was OK with me but Mummy might think it would be yukky 'cause there are germs. Will you mind, Mummy?'

I grinned. 'No, I won't mind even if he does have germs. In fact I think we might do it more than once. You see, I love Nick.'

'That's nice, Mummy. Cause so do I.'

It was obvious that she'd accepted Nick as a part of her life long ago.

Nick's Mum and Dad came in soon after. They'd been visiting a sick friend on one of the wards and confessed they thought it best to give us some time together. We talked about what had happened, though I was conscious of Miss Big Ears so I avoided the gory details.

Before they went home with Sharon, I learned a lot more from Nancy than Nick, in a fraction of the time. There was some gene missing in the brains of men when it came to disclosing information.

Once alone, I gave Nick another, more passionate kiss before interrogating him.

'Your mum told me that you and Sharon rang my parents to fill them in. It must have cost a lot, but many thanks.'

'What else would I spend my money on? Clothes?'

I considered that. Green shorts, lilac socks?

'You're right, Nick. From now on, I'll choose your wardrobe.'

'Naturally they were relieved to hear you were OK. When I explained that you'd recalled what happened with your granny, they sounded happy, if that makes sense. Told me that when they found the state you were in after being with your gran, there was an almighty row. They didn't talk to her for years afterwards. Eventually it came out that she had some sort of illness when you were there. Even so, they thought it best if you never saw her again.'

I decided it was time to share my recollections of the eight months I lived with her, presumably to keep me safe from the bombing in Manchester.

'Dad was in the forces,' I told him, 'So Mum thought it best to take me to her mother's farm near a place called Bromyard.'

It was cathartic to recall that time in Nick's sympathetic presence, I realised.

'It turns out that Granny had . . . a few issues. She hated children, she hated disorder and decided a three-year-old girl needed to learn to be quiet. She'd lock me in the cupboard under the stairs for hours on end, along with the monsters who lived there. No light, just a claustrophobic space with musty old clothes and cobwebs brushing against my skin. There must have been mothballs there too. That's why I hate the smell.

'Anyway, Mum came to visit unannounced. She might have sensed there was a problem from Granny's letters. When she saw me in rags, covered in dirt, she took me away immediately. I'd lost almost a stone in weight. Worst of all was my nyctophobia — fear of the dark. I was really screwed up. Eventually I literally shut the cupboard out of my conscious mind. The shock of the other night forced me to relive that time all over again. If it hadn't been for Pammy . . . '

'Pammy?'

'You'll think I'm mad too. My younger self. We had quite a conversation in that tunnel. She helped me with quite a few monsters I've kept with me all my life. Distrust of allowing other people get too close, for starters. After all, I once trusted Granny. I can only surmise that Sarcastic Lass was born in that stinking hole under the stairs. I can't promise that it's gong to be easy living with me but I promise it'll be worth it, lover.'

'I don't reckon you're mad at all, Pamela. We all have our monsters, though yours certainly seem scarier than any comic story I've read. Still, you have me to protect you and young Sharon now. Your days of being terrified are over.'

'If you truly mean that, my darling Mr Winters, then we must definitely toss out some of your favourite clothes.'

'Vinnies?' He was referring to the charity shop run by Saint Vincent de Paul.

I patted his cheek affectionately.

'We can try, though I suspect even they have certain standards.'

* * *

On Tuesday, Nancy and Arthur came to take me from the hospital. Arthur had taken the morning off work. Sharon was with them. Nick was teaching.

I'd spent most of Monday learning

300

how to walk with crutches. Although there was nothing broken, my lower legs and ankles were swollen and certainly tender to the touch.

I was invited to their home to rest and recuperate. When I say invited, it was more of an order.

'Please accept assistance when it's offered, Pamela. You've been through a lot. It even made the morning papers.'

'No photos of me laid up in hospital, I hope. I was out of it for awhile.'

'Your name, and a description of the destruction caused by that vile man. From what your mate, Brenda, told Arthur and me, I have to admire your strength of character. I did misjudge you and for that I'm truly sorry. Nick loves you and young Sharon. That's good enough for me.'

'I love him too, Nancy. Just took me a while longer to admit it. As for Sharon, I can't thank you and Arthur enough for taking care of her.'

'It was no problem. Between you and me, I was glad of the company. With

Arthur and Nick working, it gets lonely here. Sharon has been a great help, haven't you, dear? Shelling peas and helping me in the garden and Arthur with his veggie patch. Mrs de Luca has called over, too. She's invited me and His Nibs over for dinner tomorrow.'

'She's a lovely person. Missing her family.'

'Apparently they're coming home from Italy in a few weeks. There's one thing I must ask you about having tea with her. She said we were having spaghetti. Surely she wouldn't be giving us a Heinz 57 can for our tea?'

I laughed, before putting her mind at rest. Mrs de Luca's Spaghetti Bolognese would be a wonderful experience for them. After that, who knew what they might try next? Perhaps pizza?

★　★　★

I was able to dispense with the crutches for the carol singing on Thursday evening. The word had gotten around the other carollers, who were very supportive. However I decided to leave it until Friday before visiting the Santa's Train for the first time since the incident.

Brenda was waiting to give me any moral support I might need. Sharon rode with us on her own special trip to speak to Santa in his grotto. She was clutching her list of three requests for pressies. I'd helped her write it. She insisted on giving him a list because, as she said, 'Santa's very, very old, Mummy. If I just tell him, he might forget.'

Approaching the Train and tunnel was difficult at first. However Sharon's joy and eagerness to find the 'bestest' seats soon dissipated any terrors I might have felt.

It was Friday the twenty-second of November, yet Christmas had well and truly arrived at Waratah World. Festive music from pop to traditional carols played unobtrusively over speakers and the entire centre was decorated with tinsel and fairy lights.

As for Santa's Train, I could sense the expectation all around the crowded open carriages. I crossed my fingers.

The first scene appeared as we turned a corner from the semi-darkness into Christmastown. The cool air was one thing, yet it was the gentle flurry of snow that captivated the audience. Children and adults gasped in amazement as they reached out to touch the falling flakes.

'Mummy! Mummy. We're there,' said Sharon.

'Where, sweetheart?' I asked, wiping a tear from my cheek.

'The North Pole.'

* * *

That first scene allowed the Train passengers to suspend their belief for a few precious minutes. We passed the North Pole scene with polar bears, Arctic owls and very confused penguins, on to reindeer fields with Rudolph and his flashing nose, eventually coming up to Santa's workshop. Mrs Claus was reading mail in the penultimate scene then finally in Santa's grotto, elves helped us down to speak to jolly old Santa himself.

While Sharon took her place in line, Brenda told me of the unprecedented success of my vision.

'Are you positive you'll be ready to return on Monday?' she inquired. I assured her, I was, expecting to resume my old temporary contract.

'That's not possible, Pamela. HJ wouldn't extend it.'

I was surprised and a little crest-fallen. Perhaps Gwen could help me out with her production company, even though it was further away.

'Dave's full-time permanent position is available, though. It would be difficult for him to manage from Long Bay Prison. What do you say? A higher salary, of course. But I require an answer now. Waratah World is keen for our firm to start planning with an Easter display.'

I hugged her closely, wincing only a little at the continuing pain.

'Yes, you bet, okey-dokey, definitely, I accept . . . '

'If you're not quite sure, now Pamela . . . ' Brenda grinned back.

On the way home, I considered my early Chrissie pressies; a better paid job, my love life sorted. There was only one thing left on my own Santa list. And that would be the hardest of them all to obtain.

★   ★   ★

Over the following weeks life became very hectic, though with Nick always there by my side, it was wonderful. Even so, December brought hot weather. When I say 'hot', I mean sweating-five-minutes-after-a-shower, fry-eggs-on-the-pavement hot. Thank goodness our Santa was in the air-conditioned comfort of Waratah World.

Early December saw the three of us being invited for lunch with Nancy and Arthur. Sharon was in another room with Nick, playing some card game called Snap.

I told them that my parents were coming to visit for an extended holiday. 'When my Granny died, they inherited a lot of money.'

'Was that the woman who locked you up all day?' asked Nancy, bristling.

'Yes, unfortunately. My mother's mother. They never forgave her for that but she wanted to make amends for the hell she put me through. She missed out on seeing her grandchildren grow up. In retrospect, it could have been prevented. She was in a bad place mentally when I stayed with her, although no one suspected that.'

'Having Sharon around is almost like having a grandchild of our own. She's livened our days up so much, Pamela.'

We were all seated in the telly room,

the roller blinds drawn to keep the sun's heat out.

It was now or never.

'You do have a grandchild of your own. His name is Liam.'

Both Nancy and Arthur sat forward. Arthur spoke first. 'We'd prefer you not to mention his or Carol's name in this house, Pamela. Nick should have explained that,' he said, gruffly.

'He did. I wanted to explain that they should be part of your lives again. Nick and I see them quite a lot. I have a photo.'

I put it on the table in the middle of us. Arthur ignored it and stood up.

'Carol disappointed us. She became pregnant out of wedlock, young lady. You are overstepping your friendship with us. Don't you agree, Nancy? Nancy . . . '

But Nancy had the photo in her hands, tears misting her eyes. She sniffled and wiped her eyes.

'No, Arthur. I don't agree. You and I have been hypocrites for far too long.'

She moved to his side and handed him the photo. He took it reluctantly.

'The days I've spent sitting here crying, longing to see her again. And our grandson. Then I dry my face before shutting them out of our lives because of some doctrine that condemns women who make one mistake. It's not fair on Carol and our grandson any longer. And it's definitely not fair on me.

'Nick,' she called out. 'Get in here. You need to hear this.' Nick came in and sat by my side. I'd told him what I'd intended to do, and he'd agreed, even though it revealed his secret meetings with Carol.

Nancy moved to the mantelpiece where a baby photo of Nick sat in its frame. It had been coloured by a professional photographer.

'Nick. We've always explained that you were born early.'

'A premmie. Yeah. That's what you told everyone.'

Nancy turned to us. Arthur was now

examining the photo of Carol and Liam I'd taken not two weeks earlier.

'Well, you weren't premature. I became pregnant with your father and we chose to wed. It was during the war. If he hadn't stood by me, I would have been the outcast that Carol is now. It's time to ask her to forgive us, Arthur. It's time to let her back into our lives with open arms. And if you won't welcome them, I pity you.'

Arthur stood to embrace his wife. The photo fluttered to the table.

'She looks so sickly, Nancy. I can't believe that we've done that to our sweet Carol.' Then he went to a cupboard under the home-made television set and removed half a dozen photos of Carol as a baby, her and Nick as children, then her in a school uniform and as a young woman. He arranged them carefully back where, I assumed, they'd once been.

I prayed that Carol could return to being the healthy, happy person they'd once shared their lives with.

It would be difficult for all of them — building bridges, admitting you've been wrong then starting once more.

I asked Nick to drop me home soon after that. It had been decided by Arthur and Nancy that he'd collect Carol and Liam, then take them back to the family home. Judging by what had been said, the reconciliation would work — but only time would tell. I'd done my best. It was up to the five of them from this point onwards.

15

It was Christmas, 1969. Everywhere was closed as families celebrated the birth of Our Lord. Nick, Sharon and I went to church together, rejoicing with many of the same carols we'd been singing at the Waterfall Fountain these past few Thursday nights.

Nevertheless, by ten-thirty it was stinking hot. Sharon was methodically unwrapping her gifts, showing delight at each. It was lovely to see her excitement.

There were a lot of them, including a talking Barbie in a coral-coloured bikini which Father Christmas had placed with all the other gifts under the tree. He'd visited last night and left a note thanking Sharon for the iced Vo-Vo bikkies.

When asked why she was taking such care with the wrapping paper, Sharon calmly explained that it was so she could re-wrap them to reopen at Nancy's and Arthur's. In a strange way, it made perfect sense.

Having Mum and Dad here on this special day was unbelievable. They'd arrived two weeks before and were staying in my spare bedroom, before leaving on an extended journey to explore Australia. I was shocked the first time they accused me of sounding Australian myself, although I did realise I was copying Nick's strange abbreviation of every second word.

'Hurry up and get your new frock on, Sharon,' I said. 'We're having lunch with Nick's parents this arvo.'

'Goodness, Pamela. What's wrong with calling it 'afternoon'? Arvo indeed. Where did we go wrong?' said Mum with a smile. My parents had met Nick's parents a few times already and were becoming close friends. They liked Nick, too, although Dad did comment once about grown men wearing shorts to school.

We'd taken them out to the Blue Mountains only to find our special camping ground at Glenbrook had been devastated by bushfires. Sharon and I had been sad, until Nick explained that many plants in Australia had seeds that only germinated after a fire.

'It's the cycle of life, Pamela.'

Already, two weeks after the fires, some seeds were germinating. I guessed it was the same with me. Granny Balitsky had almost destroyed my mind once — but now I was free of my fear of the dark forever.

★   ★   ★

We arrived at the Winters' home soon after one o'clock. The cicada chorus from the surrounding trees was loud, in spite of the oppressive heat. It was touching one hundred degrees; a typical upside-down Chrissie Day. Although the trip over was stifling, once inside it was a pleasant sixty-five degrees thanks to Bruce's gift to us; a newly installed air-conditioning unit.

My mum, Nancy and I went to the kitchen to finish preparing our anticipated feast; a blend of Australian cold meats and salads along with the more traditional British cooked meal. It was a sign of things to come in terms of mixing cultures from other sides of the world.

Considering that Carol and Liam were there too, it was quite a challenge to pack everyone, dining table and the food into the converted lounge area but I was positive it would be worth it. Carol was already in much better health and both Nancy and Arthur now doted on little Liam, judging by the gifts that they'd showered on him and Carol earlier this morning.

The meal was a brilliant success, even though Nick insisted on reading out all the jokes in the Christmas crackers a second time. Outside the window in our air-conditioned room, the large thermometer read one hundred and five degrees. Everyone was watching for the expected change to arrive soon.

'We took Liam to your Train display again yesterday, Pamela. He loved it,' said Arthur. 'Made us wonder how you can top that for next Christmas?'

I finished my pavlova, the second helping of dessert I'd had. I loved the taste, especially with passion fruit on top. I was so stuffed, as was everyone else at the table. Nancy leaned over to brush a crumb from my mouth.

Mum and Dad had taken Sharon through the tunnel a few times too, although I suspected they were grateful more for the relief from the Sydney heatwave we'd experienced all week.

'To be honest, I hadn't given it a thought. Maybe Santa's Plane? I'm just glad this year was a success. My employer has picked up a number of new contracts from my little vision, apparently.'

We chatted and laughed amiably, everyone keeping an eye on the time.

There was a special television programme that was being shown at five o'clock and none of us wanted to miss it. Finally, Nick, my dad and Arthur began to clear away the mountain of dishes. Carol insisted on helping too, as did Sharon.

As they stood up, Arthur turned to Nick.

'You forgot to mention, son. What pressies did Santa bring you this morning?'

'Santa only brings gifts to children, Dad. But I did receive some wonderful music albums plus boring . . . er, I mean sedate shirts from Pamela. Oh, and a car wash kit from Sharon, bless her.'

'And what did you buy for Pamela and Sharon?' asked Nancy, giving me a sly wink.

'Nick brought me some really neat paints and a drawing toy called a siro . . . sir . . . '

'A Spirograph, sweetheart,' I said.

'You make pretty patterns with it,' said Sharon.

'Pamela?'

'It's a surprise apparently. Nick told me that he'd give me it later, whenever later is.' I gave him a playful dirty look, before checking my watch. 'Come on. Ten minutes until showtime.'

Arthur switched on the telly so the valves could warm up, then hurriedly helped in clearing the table so we could rearrange the seats and chairs.

The special Christmas edition of *Skippy* was billed in the TV Times as one of the highlights of the festive programmes — unless you liked cricket and more cricket, which I didn't.

Mum and Dad hadn't yet seen the world's most intelligent kangaroo in action, so it would be a double treat for them.

We all sat, mesmerised, for the next thirty minutes, sometimes cheering or clapping as Skippy helped rescue Santa. The biggest cheers came at the end though, when a helicopter landed and Sharon, with me by her side, clambered down to meet Skippy and his friends.

Arthur switched off the telly as the skies began darkening.

'Was that thunder?' asked Carol. The sound reverberated as lightning raced across the sky.

'Looks like the Southerly Buster has finally arrived,' Arthur declared. 'Shall we all go out the back? It should be cooler now.'

He explained to my mum and dad about the famous weather phenomenon. The winds were blowing briskly and the temperature had dropped twenty degrees as the first huge raindrops began to fall. It had moved up the coast from the south, channelled by the Great Dividing Range.

Within minutes there was a deluge. The apricot, peach and mandarin trees at the end of the garden were no longer visible. The din of thunder and rain on the galvanised iron veranda roof was deafening. I heard Nick asking if I wanted my present yet. I nodded distractedly, enjoying the spectacular downpour.

'Pamela?' I heard him speak again, as he tugged on my frock. Annoyed, I turned. He was kneeling by my side. Everyone was watching us.

'Pamela Grant. Will you do me the honour of agreeing to be my wife?'

He passed me a small, satin covered-box which he flipped open. Inside, despite the lack of sunlight, I could see the glint of light from a faceted diamond.

My knight in shining armour was asking me to marry him. My gift from my very own Saint Nick.

I lifted the ring from the box and placed it on my finger, only then answering his question.

'Yes.'

As for his dream of three brothers or sisters for Sharon, that would have to be negotiated, woman to man as equals. I was certain we could come to an agreement. Right now, I decided a long kiss was called for . . . and then some more pavlova.

Purely to celebrate, of course.

We do hope that you have enjoyed reading this large print book.

Did you know that all of our titles are available for purchase?

We publish a wide range of high quality large print books including:
**Romances, Mysteries, Classics
General Fiction
Non Fiction and Westerns**

Special interest titles available in large print are:
**The Little Oxford Dictionary
Music Book, Song Book
Hymn Book, Service Book**

Also available from us courtesy of Oxford University Press:
**Young Readers' Dictionary
(large print edition)
Young Readers' Thesaurus
(large print edition)**

For further information or a free brochure, please contact us at:
**Ulverscroft Large Print Books Ltd.,
The Green, Bradgate Road, Anstey,
Leicester, LE7 7FU, England.
Tel:** (00 44) **0116 236 4325**
Fax: (00 44) **0116 234 0205**

SOMETHING'S BREWING

Wendy Kremer

When Kate's job as a superstore manager comes to an abrupt end, she takes a risk and signs the lease to a seafront café. After hiring a teenage girl to work weekends, Kate is shocked to learn that her uncle is Ryan Scott, her former boss. He's tall, dark, attractive — and in Kate's opinion, arrogant. As she opens for business, she begins to see a different side to him. But with a café to run, Kate doesn't have time to think about Ryan, or any other man . . .